Private Justice

A Novel by

Richard Sand

Printed in Canada

For information address:
Durban House Publishing Company, Inc.
7502 Greenville Avenue, Suite 500, Dallas, Texas 75231
214.890.4050

Library of Congress Cataloging-in-Publication Data
Richard Sand, 1943

Private Justice / by Richard Sand

Library of Congress Catalog Card Number: 00-2001096198

p. cm.

ISBN 1-930754-16-7

First Edition

10 9 8 7 6 5 4 3 2 1

Visit our Web site at
http://www.durbanhouse.com

Book design by:
B[u]y-the-Book Design—Madeline Höfer & Jennifer Steinberg

For Susan

THANK YOU to Robert Middlemiss, Inspector Tony Pace, Carol Gittelman, and Jimmy Orr

Consider what you think justice requires, and decide accordingly. But never give your reasons; for your judgment will probably be right, but your reasons will certainly be wrong.

William Murray, Earl of Mansfield

Private Justice

1

There was a picture on the front page of *The New York Post* of Kirk and Lucas Rook receiving their gold shields. The idea had come from the higher-ups. "Good PR," someone downtown said.

They had gone through the Academy together and walked the same beat. For a while they even rode the same blue and white before Kirk got transferred acrosstown and Luke sent up to Washington Heights. They dated sisters, and Kirk married the smiling one, whose name was Ann.

On the day Kirk was shot to death outside The Sephora Club, his twin came rushing down. The lights on his unmarked flashing, his siren screaming, Lucas Rook knowing that death was coming and fearing it more than his own.

"I won't be there to see him go," said Lucas over and over as he came roaring down, screeching to a halt to see the mirror of himself laying in the spreading pool of blood.

But Mercy gave a final gift and for one last time they both still breathed. Lucas Rook held his brother to him. No word was said until he let him go.

"An ugly business," spoke the ranking officer on the scene.

"Anybody would have taken him for me," was all the survivor said.

He turned in his badge after his twin brother was laid to rest by white-gloved hands. In the crucible of that moment, Lucas Rook began his cruel pursuit.

Each one died who had caused that mirrored death. Some in daylight, some in stealth. The last one dragged in front of The Sephora Club.

But the tie remained between the two of them who had played cowboy games and dated sisters and who had walked the beat and rode the same blue and white and received their gold shields on the same day. Mysterious, luminiscent, offering no comfort. One twin a phantom up ahead, a pale shadow in an empty room. And Lucas Rook now at the hire of strangers, and with a need for revenge that had not left.

Rook wanted to look at the scene before he met with his potential client. He wanted to get the feel of where the little girl was dropped like a bag of rocks. He traveled Route 3 both east and west before he stopped and walked back to the flowered cross. It was next to the sign for Manoa Road where the two-lane road became a bridge over an abandoned railroad track.

Almost a year had passed since Heather Raimondo was found in a burlap bag by the side of the road. Friends and relatives still came to keep the blooms alive on the makeshift monument. Rook knew better, that soon enough the fresh flowers would be replaced by plastic ones and then by none at all.

Then the abduction and murder of Heather Raimondo would exist only in the tortured minds of the little girl's parents and by the killer's souvenirs. Rook wondered if the murderer kept a scrapbook or a lock of hair. The police file would be put away in a cardboard box. Perhaps the family would keep her room the way it was.

Rook walked along the shoulder of the road and then back into the overgrown brush and bushes, pushing aside some brambles and low-growing poison ivy with his cane. The sun was beginning to go down and the mosquitoes coming up as he made his way across the two-lane highway. The view from that side of the road and bridge was the same, but up about a hundred yards he found a small path into the weeds and brambles. There was a semi-circle of bricks three high and a half dozen beer cans. College boys or dead-end men with dead-end jobs.

He had walked a hundred scenes like this. Sometimes he'd find a piece of physical evidence relevant to a case. More often than not, just debris of everyday life that meant nothing, a popsicle stick, a torn-up book, pieces of a discarded lunch. But always there was a feeling that he carried with him when he walked the scene. The odd combination of his practiced dispassion and the feeling that evil was close by.

Rook wondered why the killer hadn't thrown his bag of death over the bridge. There was high grass on the railroad underneath and a low fog that hung like cigarette smoke. Perhaps he didn't have the time, or perhaps in his insane mind he didn't want to hurt the little girl. A bat swooped down to feed as Rook crossed back again to get his car. As he drove away, the sky had turned to asphalt and there was no moon.

2

It had been a loser day for homicide detective, Jimmy Salerno. Another iron weight dropped into the acid in his stomach. And when the day was over, he couldn't sleep. Jimmy turned over on his back, but got his acid reflux and had to take a Zantac and some Tums. He watched the clock until it was time to get up. Carmella was a heavy sleeper and didn't stir as he left for work.

When Salerno got to the station house that morning, he saw the new guy going upstairs. It was crap that the new guy was going upstairs to Administration. They could have sent somebody from his squad.

It was just another loss, Salerno told himself. Politics was always losses. Police work was getting full of them. Call for back-up and get a lady dwarf who can't speak English. The job was tough enough, pushing good men to the bottle and wrecking marriages like his partner's. It was all getting old and it was taking him with it.

Like the job, the neighborhood was going bad. His precinct wasn't a battleground yet, but it was changing fast. The wolves were showing up. Fuck the directives, the squad cars stopped them on sight. Everybody, including the detectives, drove border patrol when they were coming on or going off their shift.

4

The politics, things not being the same, losing, made not closing a case a heavier load in the shit storm the world had become. Like the murder of that little girl last year. They didn't have a lead and Jimmy Salerno knew that any case they hadn't closed in ninety days would probably stay unsolved forever. Like the dead little girl he found his first day on the force. Salerno had never gotten over that.

It was in the vestibule of a candy store the day after Christmas. She had turned blue and was frozen solid. Even the blood running down her legs was frozen. She was lying face down with her coat over her head. He had thought it was a pile of rags when he went over to check the door. Two rats were in that rag pile which had been a little girl named Helen Kocinzki, who had been raped and strangled. He had never forgotten those two rats or the girl's name, or the way her face looked when he turned her over. Frozen in fear, frozen in death.

They caught the child-killer, but he walked because a newspaper reporter, an outsider, had contaminated the crime scene. Jimmy Salerno had never forgotten that either.

There were three kinds of cases: the ones you got on quick and closed quick, the ones that kind of went away to be replaced by others and then there was this kind. The Heather Raimondo kind, the kind that didn't get cleared and no matter how faraway it got stored in cardboard boxes on basement shelves, it never left.

Salerno still had the Heather Raimondo murder book at home. Too many nights he sat up reading the newspaper accounts, notes of the patrolman on the scene, forensics, his own observations and conclusions. He read them over and over again. He must have read them a hundred times, looking for something, anything that he might have missed.

"The new guy didn't say hello or anything?" Chick Misher, asked as they loaded their bags into the trunk of the Crown Victoria. Salerno's partner was tall and well dressed. His still blond hair made him look younger than his hard fifty-one years. "He passed me in the squad room yesterday, Jimmy. He gave me a nod on his way up to Administration."

"A fucking nod, Chick?" Jimmy underhanded the keys to his partner.

"A nod. Like he was one of them little German Shepherd dog things the Ricans have in the back of their Chevy's."

"Watch it, Chick. You're gonna get written up behind that."

"Correct, James. I mean Hispanic Americans of the Caribbean derivation."

Salerno turned in his seat so he could reach the roll of mints in his pocket.

"You alright?" his partner asked him.

"Just counting the months until sunny Florida," Jimmy answered.

"I heard that." Chick made a hard right into the Dunkin' Donuts.

"A plain and a tea, no sugar," Salerno told him.

They had talked about it before, how tea was harder on the stomach than coffee, but when Jimmy ordered tea, Chick knew that something was eating at him bad.

Misher came back with the coffee, tea, and donuts, "You alright?"

Jimmy told him, "It's the Raimondo job, Chick." They tried not to think of her as a child. "It's still up on the board in my head. No way I'm going to leave that case open."

Misher knew it was an open sore. "We'll grab him up, put a noose around his neck, a round in his head, and a stake in his heart."

The two detectives said nothing more until they got to the private golf course. It was well maintained for the executives who used it and had an almost artificial-looking green. Holes six to fourteen were arguably within the sector of the precinct's responsibility.

Chick pulled up onto the side street and the two of them came through the woods, startling the golfers at the tee. One of the foursome was about to say something when he noticed the weapon that Misher carried "cross-draw" style inside his waistband.

Jimmy was a bit more discreet, covering his service revolver by wearing his shirt outside of his pants. He was no less a startling figure, however, shaped like a fireplug the way he was with his trousers rolled up to the calf and his high black socks showing.

"Everything alright?" the lawyer in the group asked.

The dentist noticed the two invaders carried clubs. "You gentlemen want to play through?"

Chick tipped his Panama and hit his tee shot up the center of the fairway.

Salerno looked more like a catcher than a golfer. He adjusted the .38 revolver that he wore pancake style at his back and drove the ball deep into the woods. He was about to start the hole over when his beeper went off. "It's the boss, Chick."

"Why do you bring that when we're golfing?"

"'To protect and serve'. We'll call in from the clubhouse."

"Certainly, partner, certainly," Chick said. "We have work to do. Five more holes' worth."

7

Misher kept hitting them straight. Salerno kept hitting them far. As they approached their final hole, Jimmy announced, "We're even. The loser explains to the Inspector where we've been." He boomed his tee shot which hooked to the left.

Chick smiled. "You're on."

Salerno's beeper went off again. "Christ, his hemorrhoids must be bleeding," he said.

"He rides that stationary bike like he's a maniac, Jimmy, and then he sits on that foam donut."

The detectives finished their last hole. Misher called in even though he had won.

"I beeped a half hour ago," the Inspector said.

"We're on our way, boss."

"Two jobs came in while you two were on safari, Chick. You're up next so you caught one. Only I'm switching it to your partner. You get an assault on a school teacher by some prosty. I don't know if the teacher is her john or what. I'm giving the other job to Salerno. Another one of them kids, a dump job like the last one. I'll fill you in when you get back to the house, which I trust will be shortly."

"We're on our way, boss. Protect and Serve." Misher relayed the conversation to Jimmy, who pushed his driving hard. They went straight to the Inspector's office, Salerno stopping only for the clip-on tie in his desk.

Inspector Joe Zinn was a thin, graying man with a neat moustache. He was animated and walked around his office when he spoke. "Jimmy, the case is yours. We're keeping this off the board until we know what we got. I'll take care of that. If anybody asks, you're still working the Raimondo case. The new job is at the very end of Andorra Woods, another dump job, another little girl. No rigor. No clear cause of death."

Salerno took his tie off and went to the scene.

8

Being on the job for all those years had taught Detective Salerno to keep focused on what he was doing. But as he drove out Henry Avenue, he could not help remembering Heather Raimondo and Helen Kocinzki. The things he might have done. The cases he didn't clear. The battles he had lost.

Salerno took out his long reporter's pad as he got out of his unmarked and wrote down his mileage. The police officer on the scene was named Carlos Rodriguez. Salerno took his name and badge number, the location, and the time of arrival. Rodriguez was pacing back and forth.

Jimmy pulled on the latex gloves from his pocket. "What we got here, patrolman?"

"A little girl. Around here behind the tree. I didn't touch nothing. She's behind the tree. I was first on the scene. Sanitation called it in. They were emptying the cans around the playground over here. Dispatch sent me. I called my sergeant. I didn't touch nothing. I protected the scene."

Fine," Salerno told him. "Why don't you wait over there?" He motioned to one of the cement benches. "Catch a smoke, Rodriguez. Whistle when the wagon comes."

Rodriguez choked when he spoke, "The dogs or whatever got at her some."

"Okay, patrolman. I got it. Watch your perimeter, and let me know when the meat wagon gets here." Salerno made a note to call the dispatcher and the sergeant to see if Rodriguez had told them anything else.

Jimmy walked the area. The grass had been cut recently, but the people from Crime Scene would still have it combed. Anything at all would be put in plastic bags. "Police your smoke? We don't want your DNA at the scene."

"I'm sorry. I'll tell you when the Medical Examiner arrives."

Salerno went over to the body of the little girl. She was lying face down against a large oak tree with a root system that pushed through and went over ground. He walked out a hundred feet and then came back slowly in concentric circles, snapping photos with his Instamatic as he did. Crime Scene would do the same, but with a better camera. There was nothing of interest on the ground except a rubber band, two beer bottles and three cigarette butts. He bagged them all.

The detective walked back over to the body. The girl looked like a big doll lying on her side. She was in a white terrycloth robe as if someone had just bathed her and gotten her ready for bed. He wondered whether that was the killer's intention or whether she was in terrycloth because you couldn't get prints off of that. Her hair was black. She wore one patent leather shoe. The scavengers, dogs or whatever, had gotten at her. For a crazy moment he saw the body of Heather Raimondo and then of Helen.

Salerno had seen dead kids before and had a dozen close-ups in his murder book from the Raimondo job, but he knew it would not protect all of him. Nothing ever did. He had to protect himself by shutting down. Jimmy took a deep breath and touched her. The body was cold. When he turned the body over, he saw an angelic face with a bloody wound where her nose belonged.

He checked the little girl's body for marks or stains, but there weren't any. There were no fluids underneath and no maggots. Salerno checked the body again and took more notes and photos. Then he heard a van pull up, the technicians arriving to do the scene, and right behind them was the Medical Examiner.

Rodriguez was still there, but had forgotten to tell Salerno when the wagon arrived. Jimmy walked over to him. "I thought I told you to tell me when the wagon got here, patrolman."

Rodriguez gazed back at him blankly.

"Go home and get some sleep or whatever," Salerno said. "Hug your kid."

"Sorry, detective. I never seen something like this before."

"Get used to it," Salerno said. "You'll be seeing this one for quite a while."

Gerry Doto was the crime tech and he was a good one "I hate these jobs. Kids I mean. It's never quite right. Me, I'm supposed to leave on 'vacay' tonight, you know, with the wife. It's lucky us getting off at the same time." He opened his box and put on his gloves. "You find anything?"

Salerno handed over the trash he had picked-up. "You find anything that I didn't, you'll call me."

"Sorry, Jimmy, like I said, we're flying down to the sunny climes." He performed a quick cavity search on the little girl. "Somebody'll call. I'll leave them a note."

The driver from the M.E. started over, a thin black man with a large afro. Salerno waved him off. "What could you do to move this for me, Gerry?"

Doto was combing out the girl's hair. "Helluva wound here, took her little button nose right off. I'll see what I can do for you, Jimmy." He motioned to the driver. "Tag her and bag her, Jamal. I gotta roll."

3

The Inspector wanted to go for his run before Salerno got back in from the scene. His "run", was a walk to and around the diamond-shaped park eight blocks from the station house. It calmed him down. He needed that because his blood pressure was up again.

Zinn had engineered a system for his precinct, a system that had taken him years to perfect. When that system was followed, things went smoothly. But he had no patience when that system was ignored. Just the week before, he had been at Misher for trying to switch shifts so he could take some accumulated leave.

"You know I hate that!" the Inspector had said. "Things work because they're in workable order. They're in workable order because we have rules. Rules are rules. That's why we got them."

Now Joe Zinn found himself compromising that system by giving the new job to Salerno and that made his pressure rise. He needed to get out for his run, but he also needed to be in his office. Even though he knew he would pay the price, he locked the door and got on his exercise bike.

As he pedaled on, the Inspector thought about the new DOA and the Raimondo case. That case still hadn't been cleared. There were no leads.

Joe called his daughter at work. "Just to tell you I love you," he said. "You need anything?" Then he called home, but the wife was out shopping. "It's nothing," he told the answering machine. "I've got a busy day. I'll call you back."

The Inspector put on a clean white shirt in his small white bathroom and eased himself down onto the rubber donut on his chair. There was a knock on the door. He could see through the frosted glass that it was Vanessa Esposito, his Information Officer.

He didn't want her to come in when he was sitting on that cushion.

"It's me, Inspector, Esposito. I'm here for the meeting."

"Very good, Lieutenant. You're early. I'll buzz you."

"Thanks, boss," she replied. "I'm good to go."

He smiled at her use of the military term. Hard worker and a great ass, the Inspector said to himself.

Detective Misher had been downstairs talking to the desk sergeant. He came in as his partner was taking his necktie from the middle drawer of his desk.

"You going to a wedding?"

"I'm wearing a tie for eight years when I'm going to the boss's meeting. You probably sleep in a fucking tie, partner."

"Armani."

"This is not going to be a good meeting," Salerno said. "Joe's been riding his stationary bike like a maniac. His ass is to going to be killing him."

Chick pulled on the cuffs of his blue dress shirt so they showed the appropriate amount below his sports jacket. "We'll hear about his 'roids and fissures for the next two weeks."

Esposito came up to the two detectives. Her black hair and blue eyes gave her a striking appearance. Even though she just made the departmental height requirement, her figure was, as Chick had appropriately described it, "very well formed".

Misher started to say something about her walk, but Jimmy cut him off. "Let's get this done," he said.

The three of them went up to the door with the frosted glass. Salerno knocked.

"Come," Inspector Zinn told them.

"That's an order, Esposito," Chick added under his breath.

Zinn was standing when they entered his office. He was in obvious discomfort.

"Let's get going, people." Then he realized they were a chair short. "Chick, will you get a chair from the squad?"

"I'll get one, boss," Esposito said. She went out to roll one in for herself.

"Great view," Misher remarked.

"Abundanza," Salerno added.

The Inspector cleared his throat. When Esposito came back in, he started. "What do we got, Jimmy?"

"What we got here is another dead girl," Salerno said. Esposito winced. "We don't know who she is. She could be one of them milk carton kids."

"What I don't want is a line of publicity," Inspector Zinn told them. "I don't want a panic. I don't want publicity. I don't want the Feds. Of the five thousand or so kids that are reported missing each year in our lovely city, three quarters are cleared fast and almost all of the rest are runaways. I don't want the citizens having nightmares. I want a tight lid on this until we hear from the Medical Examiner."

The Inspector shuffled some papers on his desk. Then he turned to talk to the three of them again. "People, if you find that any of this gets around outside of this office I want it cleared up immediately. I don't want it on the '24's'. This will not appear on the list of today's crimes as we do not yet know if we have one."

"I'll talk to the patrol officer, boss, Salerno said. "He was pretty shaken up. He needs some TLC."

"Maybe Esposito could help," Chick added.

"With what, Detective?" she said.

The Inspector waved his hands. "Please don't go 'Human Relations' on me, people," he told them.

"It's alright, boss," Esposito answered.

"Chick, I want you to back up Jimmy on this. I want you to find out who the DOA is. Cross-check this with Missing Persons. Try what's-her-name in Juvenile Aid. Maybe she's got something."

"Esposito," the Inspector went on, "see if there are any press calls on this. Answer them if they've called twice, but tell them zero. I may want your involvement in the ID. If we come up with nothing, I want you to try the National Child Safety Council. They do those milk cartons. Use an indirect approach. You're a reporter or something. And whoever sends out those little blue flyers."

Esposito nodded, "That's ADVO, boss. They're from Connecticut," she answered. "They send out about seventy-five million flyers a week. They don't find all that many. There's also the National Center for Missing and Exploited Children in Virginia,"

"Negative on that. What I don't want is the Feds in here. Those college boys at the Bureau's Child Abduction Unit, not to mention Assistant Special Agent In Charge Epps. He busted our balls last time. They came up with nothing. We do *not* want the FBI in here. I'm sure you'll perform in your usual thorough manner, Esposito," Zinn nodded to her.

She knew that her part of the meeting was over. "Thanks, Inspector," she answered. "And it will be a pleasure working with these two fine detectives." She walked out smartly.

"Bitches with badges," Misher commented under his breath.

Joe Zinn sat back down on his donut, trying to stifle the expression of his pain. "If the Feds think we got multiple cases, they'll be up here in a flash. Epps gives me a pain right where I'm sitting. Last time, he's reading me protocol—how we're supposed to write up any missing kid that turns up DOA as a kidnaping. I told him his census must be down and to sit by the phone. I'll call him when I need him, the smug redhead Ivy League prick. I was grabbing up them predators when he was still wearing pajamas with a trap door in the back. And the papers and all will be straining at the leash to drag out the 'Marie Noe' case again. No way anybody kills eight kids and walks now."

The Inspector adjusted himself on the foam pillow.

"Jimmy, what do we have?"

Salerno took out his notebook, but just as a prop. He knew what little there was to know about this case. "We got the scene slowed down," he began. "We got it taped off—but there were two Sanitation guys. We'll catch them at the taproom on the clock so they won't remember a thing.

"What I got from me eyeballing," he went on, "is that it's a homicide. There was no fluid under her, so I don't think she was done there. No rigor or maggots so the crime and the drop were pretty recent. There was no obvious cause of death. The dogs whatever got at her feet and her face. Toolmarks is supposed to get back to me on the face wound just to make sure.

"Like the Raimondo case, there were no insertions, no

rubber balls, butterflies, or whatever, so I don't think it's a rape fantasy. I got no prints. We'll look for latents. She was in a terrycloth robe. Maybe the doer knows what he's doing since that don't take prints. Maybe cleaning her up, the robe and all being some kind of whacked-off remorse. I haven't heard on any of the organics." He looked back at his notebook. "I'm meeting with Sex Crimes this afternoon."

"Maybe some kind of taunting," Misher said. "The way the body was left so public."

Salerno nodded and went on. "I don't think we got a copy cat on my case, boss. I got the feeling we got one predator instead of two. Even though in the Raimondo case, we don't have no robe. That was in the summer or the robe is some kind of what they call 'evolution.'

Inspector Zinn was making notes. "I'll allow the victim out of the system until we get an ID and get something from the Medical Examiner. Sam Nessel is alright. And, Jimmy, I want you at the autopsy. If we got a baby killer, I want a full court press, everybody from 2 Squad and 5. I'll be authorizing overtime. We'll look at everything, stealing clothes off the line-whatever."

Salerno was thinking about the autopsy. He had been at dozens and dozens, from the most detailed forensic pathology to a chop job in a makeshift garage. He knew that they needed a determination of the cause of death, but he did not look forward to seeing the little girl split open.

Joe Zinn got back up which meant their meeting was over.

Salerno drove home still wearing his clip-on tie. As was the custom, on Wednesdays, he dropped his partner off at home. Chick Misher lived at the most northwest corner of the city. In fact, the other side of the street was not even in

Philadelphia. He liked that since the Department still had a residence requirement.

"You need me to, partner, I can move some things around. We can double-team this job," Chick said.

Jimmy nodded and pulled over in front of the corner house. There was a little bit of lawn in front that Misher kept neat and well-edged. He stopped and picked up two leaves that had drifted off the tree in the front. When he looked up, Salerno was gone.

Misher went inside and changed his clothes, hanging his slacks and sports jacket in plastic garment bags. Jimmy said he could slice a bread with the crease of his pants and he wasn't far off.

Chick lived alone and liked that. He'd fry himself a couple of eggs for dinner and run the vac. There was horse racing or whatever on cable and he'd watch that. After his second beer, he'd drift off to sleep.

4

Rook drove from Heather Raimondo's dumping ground to the home of the dead girl's parents. Forty minutes was a long ride. Too long for somebody to spend with the girl in the car, alive or dead.

He drove the route back and then came in, circling the block around his destination. It was a clean family neighborhood, but the pall of the child's death was darkly present.

Rook noted that the driveway was full with two big cars parked in front. The house had good stone work and lots of white wrought iron. As he opened the door of his car, two men got up from the small porch and came to meet him in the driveway. They were large men, one with a crewcut and freckles, the other was Italian and had bad skin.

"Mr. Rook?" the Italian one asked. He pronounced it like it rhymed with "nuke." "We work for Mr. Raimondo. He'd like you to come in."

They walked alongside of the house, following the line of shrubbery and the mushroom lights that lit the way. The crewcut followed behind. "That's some car," he said. "I didn't see the emblem. What is it, some kind of big Corvette?"

"Jerry, don't be bothering Mr. Raimondo's guest," the Italian one told him.

Carlo Raimondo met them at the door. He had salt and pepper hair and wore lots of gold. "Thanks, Phil, you can wait outside. Send the kid home if you want."

They walked through a small paneled hall into the kitchen. There were two other men in the room. One of them wore an expensive suit with a french-cuffed shirt and silk tie. The other was a huge man, well under six foot, but weighing over three hundred pounds. There was a Great Dane laying under the table at the fat man's feet. When Rook came in, the dog began to get up, spilling the cups of coffee and nearly toppling the bottle of scotch.

"Jesus Christ, Sebastian!" the fat man yelled. "Lay down!" The dog complied, settling the table back to rest.

"I'm Carlo Raimondo, Mr. Rook. This is my brother, Harry. Heather's father. And this is our lawyer, Anthony Castriota."

The lawyer extended his manicured hand. He was a handsome man, but his skin looked somehow too perfect, almost as if he were wearing make-up.

"Counselor," Rook said. He shook hands with the Raimondos and took the white chair Harry Raimondo offered.

"You want coffee, a shot, maybe a cold beer, Mr. Rook?"

"Coffee would be good."

Harry fiddled with his stogie as Castriota began. "Actually, I'm here unofficially, Mr. Rook. I'm counsel to Local 1737 Operating Engineers. Cranes and what-not. Carlo here is the Local's treasurer. Heather is his niece."

"Was," Harry said without looking up.

"Let me talk for a minute, will ya, Tony," Carlo said. He fingered his heavy link bracelet as he spoke. "Mr. Rook, this ain't union business. It's family business."

"Family business or 'family' business?" Rook asked.

"If it was 'family business', we'd 've had the fucking creep's balls on a platter long before this," Harry answered. "Angela, Heather's mother, swore me to keep certain people out of this. I couldn't deny her that."

"The Feds get involved in this case?"

"We like to avoid complexities, Mr. Rook," the lawyer answered. "However, we were contacted by the Federal Bureau of Investigation. Someone named Epps, but that didn't go anywhere. The police detective in charge, James Salerno, was very committed, but they couldn't find a thing."

"Were there any suspects?" Rook asked.

Harry answered, "Salerno confided in me that they had one, but that it didn't pan out."

"What did he tell you, Harry?"

"That's all he'd say, Mr. Rook." Carlo answered. "He told us he wouldn't give me any more because the guy would have wound up hanging on a hook. Salerno still calls now and again. Don't he, Harry?"

"Yeah, he calls." Harry lit his stogie and the smell of anisette filled the room.

"What exactly do you want me to do, and who is it I'm going to be working for?"

"The Raimondo's," Castriota answered.

"By that, do you mean Harry and Angela?" Rook asked.

"For my brother," Carlo answered, "and his wife."

"Then you have got to tell me that, Harry. And you got to pay me and tell me what you want me to do."

Harry Raimondo poured himself a shot of Johnnie Walker. "I have to get 'closure', Mr. Rook. That's the word they all use. My wife, she's gone. She's here, but she's not. She's on depression pills and anxiety pills. There ain't nothing going to bring her back, neither." He swallowed the scotch and poured himself another. "Me, I've got to get the animal who killed my little girl. I've got to stand there and see him dead."

Carlo Raimondo held up his hand. "You know what he's talking about? You understand, Mr. Rook? Can you handle that?"

"If we reach an agreement. My fee is one hundred dollars an hour plus expenses. I will need a retainer of five thousand dollars. My fee will be for my direct involvement in the capture of the murderer of your daughter, Harry. This fee covers my services on a 'best efforts' basis for a period not to exceed six months. During that time period I may not be working for you exclusively. If I am successful in the first thirty days, I want a twenty-five percent bonus."

"We want you on only this job, Rook," Carlo told him.

"We will compensate you for your exclusivity", the lawyer said, admiring his cufflinks.

"I should be closing another case soon. I can't give you exclusivity until then. It should be no more than a few days."

"Your expenses, not normal operating expenses, rent, the like," Castriota added.

"Agreed. And after the initial three months, the deal can be canceled by either party," Rook said.

Carlo nodded. "Agreed."

"Harry?" Rook asked.

Harry Raimondo shook his head, but answered, "Agreed." He leaned across the table to shake Rook's hand. As he did, the dog growled. Harry kicked the Dane under the table.

"We need to talk," Rook told him.

"Tell him what he wants to know, Harry," Catriota said. "Tell him everything he wants to know."

"Alone. We need to talk alone," Rook said.

"I don't…" Castriota started, but Carlo cut him off.

"Harry, you alright with this?" Carlo asked.

"Yeah, I'm alright. Let's get this over with."

Carlo and the lawyer went into the parlor. Rook stretched out his bad leg. "Begin at the beginning, Harry."

Harry Raimondo poured them each a drink. Then he took a photo of his daughter out of his wallet and put it in the middle of the white kitchen table. "Okay, Mr. Rook. It goes like this. Angela, the wife, she used to work part time at this chiropodist's office, Dr. Braslow. You know, they call them 'podiatrists' now. She don't no more. She's on these pills, two kinds, maybe three."

"Is this the first time she's on medication?"

"What do you mean?" The big man shifted uncomfortably on the kitchen chair.

"Had she been under a doctor's treatment before or taking something?'"

"Like what? She didn't do no drugs."

Rook moved on. "Your wife…"

Raimondo looked at him.

"You were saying your wife worked part time."

"Right. We didn't need it. I didn't want her working. But it was one of them women's liv things. She don't do it no more, can't. She can't do nothing. Just sleep. Sometimes she's goofy, walking around and around and all. Talking like it never happened, goofy. Doc says it's better when she cries, but I guess her tears are all dried up."

"Who's her doctor, Harry?"

"Fenton. Been our family doctor for years." Harry reached into the drawer behind him, "You need a pen. You going to write things down, right?"

"Tell me what happened, Harry."

Raimondo was rubbing the dog's flank with his foot. "Okay, Angela takes Heather," he paused. "I mean she used to take Heather to the playground in the afternoon. She went to the pre-school in the morning on them days that Angela worked.

"Right after work they'd go to the City playground across from St. Alice's."

"Did they go alone?"

"No, they usually met Peggy Nolan at the corner and went over together." He poured himself another scotch and offered one to Rook who waved him off.

"Who's she?"

"Peggy Nolan. She's German-Irish. She got a boy who would be around Heather's age. Then they'd meet, the other mothers, I mean. I guess I should say parents because sometimes Atkins, he's the colored guy, would be there with his boy. He works shift work. His wife's a cripple."

Rook nodded for him to go on.

"He's a moolie, you know, a black guy, but he's alright. He's a fireman."

"Is there security at the playground, Harry?"

"We never needed it before. There's houses right across the street."

"Any drug use during the day or after dark?"

"No, not right across from the parish there isn't. This is a good, clean neighborhood. Look, I got to go to the bathroom. Sebastian, he's going to get up when I do. He's big so don't get startled or whatever." Harry got up and the huge dog unfolded himself from under the table and followed the fat man down the hall.

Rook used the break to look around the room. The kitchen was only partially clean. The stove had tomato stains on the enamel and there were dirty dishes in the sink.

Harry came back without the dog and started in again, "It happened so fast. Peg's kid was running to the street after his ball. Angela went after him. When she turned around, Heather was gone." He shook his head and then was quiet.

"Where was the fireman?"

"He wasn't there that day. He was at work, a shift thing. The police checked that."

"Who was there,?"

"Only Angela and Peggy with the kids."

"What was Peggy doing?"

"She was over at the swings where Heather was. Then she ran after her boy, too. And in that second…"

"Were there any ransom demands, Harry? Any contact from the kidnapper?"

"Just some crank calls after she was found. The cops said it was vultures trying to squeeze me."

Rook leaned back in the chair "Did you talk to any of them?"

"No. I let the cops handle it. A lot of good that did. You want something, Rook, a shot whatever, a glass of wine?"

"Let's get through this first. Who was on the case?"

"First, a regular cop, you know, a patrolman, came to see me. Then a woman from the Sex Crime Unit. Then these two detectives, Jim Salerno and his partner, Chuck something, his name was, although Salerno did most of everything. He said it was his case."

"When did the FBI get involved?"

They heard a car pull away from out front. Carlo came back into the kitchen. "I sent the lawyer away. He costs a fortune. I got my membership to answer to." Carlo put his hand on his brother's arm. "You alright?"

"Yeah, I'm alright, big brother."

"Good, good. I'll leave youse two. My man will come back after he drives me home. You want him to bring anything back?"

Harry shook his head and the two brothers embraced. Rook stretched his leg.

"We went to them after the police couldn't get anywhere," Harry continued. "We spoke to an Agent Epps, said he was the head guy. He said he'd get back to us, but he never did. I guess they came up with nothing or lost interest, whatever."

"Did you talk to anyone else about this?"

"My son, Frank, from my first marriage. He was away at school, at Rutgers. Frank's a good boy. He was close to my wife."

"Was?" Rook asked.

"Was, is. What's the difference? Angela was a big help to him when his mother died. It's hard for anybody to be close to him. He pushes them all away."

"When was that? When did his mother die?"

Raimondo gave Rook a hard look. "Five years ago. Ovarian cancer. It was bad for him. He was at college. Salerno checked. I told you that."

Rook nodded, "Anybody else? You deal with anybody else?"

"We contacted the Center for Missing Children. That's in Virginia. And we went to a survivors' group, but Angela couldn't stand it. Look, let's go into the parlor. This is getting all close in here." He stood and pulled down the top of his velour running suit.

Rook followed Harry down the hall. The fat man moved surprisingly well. Rook wished that he had brought his cane in from the car, but that had cost him more than one job.

The parlor was square and bright. Harry sat on the sofa and motioned Rook to the single, dark red chair.

"Did you hire anyone else before me, any private investigator?"

"No, Castriota had somebody on it, but it went nowhere."

"What's his name?"

"Ask the lawyer. I don't know. It didn't go nowhere."

"Anybody else?"

"Some reporters called. I told them to fuck off. One of them came here twice. I let the dog out after him. My wife wanted to see one of them fortune tellers, but I wouldn't let her."

Rook looked towards the picture window. Two children were running by. "How long was it before they found your daughter?"

"Two days, or really a day and a half. By the road." Raimondo reached to pet the dog that wasn't there. "There's flowers there, where they found her."

"I saw," Rook told him. "Had anything happened in the neighborhood before? Any burglaries or prowlers?"

"The police told me there were no sex criminals or nothing. Some petty crimes. I mean a car got stolen, but that was just a joy ride. They got the kid. Salerno told me he was fourteen. Like that."

"I'll check into that. Just a couple of more questions. Did you use a babysitter?"

"Two sisters, Caitlin and Elizabeth. They're twins, both sixteen, but mostly we stayed in."

"Do you have a *gumar*?" Rook rolled his r.

The fat man half-smiled. "Just cause I'm Italian doesn't mean I got someone on the side. And if I did, she weren't no part of this. And now, since Heather's gone, she's not part of nothing. It ain't right."

"Anything else you want to tell me?"

27

Raimondo offered the photograph of his daughter. It looked tiny in his hand. "You should have this if you're going to take this job."

Rook put the picture in his shirt pocket. "Nothing I'll do will bring you or your wife any peace of mind, but I'll do my best to get the killer."

"My wife is never going to be the same. Maybe me neither. And our daughter's never coming back. Maybe Frank will get married and have kids. But if I'm ever going to sleep again, I got to see that fucker dead. You know what I'm saying." He paused and made fists with his wide hands. "I need for you to get him like you got the pricks who killed your brother. My brother told me about it."

"I can't promise you that. I can only promise that when I get him, I'll call you before I call the police."

"Good enough," Raimondo said. He let his Dane back in. Together they walked out. The dog peed on the shrubbery. "I used to care about that, Mr. Rook, now I don't."

Rook's celphone rang as he walked to his car. "Did you get what you want?" Carlo asked.

"I got enough."

"He needs for it to be made even."

"I told him that if I get his daughter's killer, I'd call him before I take it to the police."

"You know what's going on here, Rook. From your own situation," Carlo Raimondo said. "You know what we want."

"And what's that?"

"Justice, Rook. We want justice."

"It's got nothing to do with what you want, Carlo." Rook started up Kirk's Avanti. "It's what your brother needs."

He swung away in the black fiberglass coupe.

28

5

Salerno took his time getting to the Medical Examiner's office. He went down by the Airport, and by Lou Turk's, which used to be a hot spot when he was just coming up, and then the long way around.

The M.E.'s was a wide, free-standing brick building with three overhead doors in the back. For a reason that no one quite understood, all police personnel were required to check their weapons at the front desk.

"Good morning, officer," the intake man said. He offered up a storage box for Salerno and gave him a red plastic token for his gun.

"It's 'detective' like I told you the last time."

The clerk gave a forced smile. "Detective," he said as he rubbed his face.

The inside of the building was painted a light green. There were two sets of doors leading into the exam rooms.

"Which one is Nessel in?"

"Dr. Nessel is in Exam Room Three," the intake man answered. "Detective" he added, rubbing his face again.

Salerno went down the hall. When he got to the door, he put a dab of Vapo-Rub in each nostril. The air lock caused by the pressured air system caused his ears to "pop" as he entered the room. "I don't like this," Salerno said to himself.

Sam Nessel was breaking up the rigor mortis in the limbs of an eighty-five-year-old black woman. "My patient doesn't like it either," he answered. "You here for the MVA, Detective Salerno? This is the pedestrian who lost to a taxi."

"I thought you were doing the girl, Doc."

"There's a face shield behind you," Nessel said. There was another cracking sound as he popped the sternum.

Salerno went over for the shield. "AIDS?" he asked.

"Who knows anymore. AIDS, TB, Hepatitis C. You want to help? Double glove." Doc Nessel made a "Y" cut down to the pelvis. "I'll get to your girl after lunch. I'm running behind."

Jimmy Salerno could hear the sounds of the M.E. removing the old woman's glands and packing them in plastic containers. "That guy who invented Tupperware was a genius. You want to wait here, or I'll meet you in the lounge down the hall?" Nessel asked.

"No hurry, Doc." The M.E.'s dictation became a buzz to Salerno. When he realized it was the sound of the cranium saw, he stepped back outside to clear his head.

The Medical Examiner removed the old lady's brain and weighed it before putting it into the little plastic tub. As a favor to the funeral director, who gave him baseball tickets, he filled the empty skull cavity with wet paper towels to keep the shape from changing.

Nessel stepped off the stool he needed to reach the table and pulled off his latex gloves. He came through the air-lock into the hall where Salerno was waiting. "We can grab a bite. If I don't get lunch early today, I probably won't get it at all. You see how backed up I'm getting."

He reached for his cigarettes and lit up. "Smoking will

kill you," he announced.

Nessel spoke as he exhaled, "I've done a preliminary external on your case. No significant wounds except the face and the one foot. They appear to be post-mortem. There's some bruising on the one arm so it looks like she could have been grabbed up. There was a slight abrasion on the forehead. No ligature marks. There appears to be no sexual activity. The tech did 'swabs and smears,' but I haven't had a chance to look at the slides. I'll redo them anyway. When I get a read on the organics, I'll let you know. There was no decomp to speak of, and rigor was just setting in. No cause of death yet."

The detective had his long, narrow reporter's pad out and was taking notes. "The wounds?"

"I'll take photos and get them over to Weapons and Toolmarks for you. I think they were probably a dog, but there could have been a couple."

"You got anything for Hairs and Fibers, Doc?"

The M.E. snubbed out his cigarette. "The hairs, appear to be two types, one on her and one on the robe. They could be anything. The victim's, your murderer's, or from the bag. One of the hairs looks like a body hair so you're not going to be able to match that anyway. The other looks like doll hair. It's not human. Clearly synthetic. You want to grab something? I got to get something into my stomach."

"I got to get back to the office, Doc. I appreciate your time. Call me if you get anything."

"You coming back? Your case will be done by tomorrow for sure."

"A copy of your report will be good."

Nessel waited for the detective to leave before he went back in. He had never gotten used to knowing that people were watching him walk.

Salerno picked up his gun at the front desk. The clerk was sitting with his hands folded, "Get a life," the detective told him.

He had brought the Heather Raimondo murder book so that he could look at it right after the autopsy. Maybe it would make something click in his head. Jimmy Salerno looked at the pages of photos and reports. Nothing happened. He left the book on the back seat of his unmarked and drove to the driving range to hit a bucket of balls before going back to the station house.

Chick Misher caught up to Salerno as he was trying to get settled back at his desk. "Lunch, Jimmy?"

"I could use a beer or six, partner."

"I heard that."

Chick drove to "Higgins." Bill Higgins had "thirty and out" on the job, and his kid worked behind the bar after having fallen off a fire escape.

Misher watched his partner thumb loose a Tums, so he tried to steer the conversation to one of their regular subjects. "Carol Moon has a great set of cans, Jimmy."

"She does that. It's a fine thing."

"It's a fine thing she does for the Department."

"For the City, Chick."

"For the State."

"For all Mankind."

"God bless Carol Moon," Salerno said.

Billy Higgins' place had a big sign over the bar: "It's Us

Against Them, Drink Up." The place was mostly empty since it was almost two o'clock. They took their usual seats. Chick liked a table by the window so he could watch the shoppers come and go from the supermarket.

"Jesus, did you see that woman?" he said. "She must have two thousand dollars worth of toilet paper. She's got two carts full."

Salerno was looking at the menu he had seen a thousand times. "It ain't right her staying in there."

"Who, Jimmy?"

"That little girl. They got her in the box for overnight."

Misher nodded. "That's not right. It's just not right."

The lunch was fast and good. Chick had the crabcake sandwich with cole slaw. Jimmy ate a bowl of chili, but skipped the onions because his heartburn had been getting him.

They finished their beers and went over to pay. Young Billy took their cash. "Tell your Dad we was asking for him," Jimmy said.

Billy smiled.

"None too swift, Young Billy, is he?" Chick said as they left.

Salerno held his hand out for the car keys. "Time for a piano lesson, partner."

"Me, I love the piano. Liberace and what-not," Chick answered.

Stewart Charles Dunmoore had very long white fingers. For that reason alone, Jimmy Salerno liked him for the unsolved murder of Heather Raimondo. Even after Dunmoore had told him that his long fingers came from years of playing the piano and Jimmy's wife had confirmed the fact that piano players did get long fingers, Salerno could not help but see them around the little girl's throats.

The two detectives drove back to the piano teacher's townhouse even though there was nothing to link him. Salerno wanted him even more now that he had seen the girl in the terry cloth robe with her nose cut off.

They arrived as Dunmoore was getting in his car to drive away. Salerno blocked his exit.

"Going somewhere, Stewart Charles? You've been at it again. Grabbing your new girlfriend, like you did Heather, by her soft white neck. I can see her little legs kicking in the air and the way she shit herself when she died."

"Did your dickie get hard when you choked her?" Chick said. "Did you go all messy-mess when she died, music teacher?"

Dunmoore sighed. The two detectives led him back to the brick-faced townhouse. When they got inside, Misher closed the blinds.

Salerno pointed to the piano. "Sit down. Play a song." Then he hit Dunmoore in the back of the head with a phone book.

Chick came over and slapped him twice across the side of his face.

The piano teacher slumped in the chair and cringed. "Why? Why?" he cried.

"Play us a song," Chick grabbed him by his long black hair and jammed his face into the piano. "I saw Jerry Lee Lewis do this once," he said. He raked the music teacher's face up and down the keys.

"Did you play for your girlfriends like that, piano man?" Salerno asked. "Did you want to make beautiful music together, you and your six-year-olds?"

When Stewart Charles lifted his head, blood was dripping from his nose and he had blood on his teeth. He started to speak, but saw his blood and started crying again.

"Go wash your faggot self up," Salerno said. "I don't want your HIV sprayed all over me and my partner."

Misher pulled on his latex gloves. "We got exposure here, partner?" he asked Jimmy.

"No, we're alright. Stewart here is having her period."

Salerno stood in the doorway of the bathroom to see that the music teacher didn't try to cut himself or take pills. Dunmoore stopped the bleeding and although he was still obviously shaken, he turned to the two detectives, "The fact that the two of you are both Nazis doesn't make me anything. Because I play the piano doesn't mean I am a homosexual, nor does the fact that I teach music mean I like little girls in the wrong way."

Salerno let him talk, hoping it would lead to something.

"We've been through all this. My lawyer told me to call him if you came back."

"Your phone's not working now," Salerno answered him. "I'll take a tour while my partner here sits with you and you can tell him all about it."

"Maybe you could play me some show tunes, dear," Chick said. "I just love Judy Garland."

"You'll have to come back with a warrant. I don't want anything walking out of here, and I don't want things falling out of your pockets. I've seen on television how that works."

"Okay, Liberace," Salerno smiled. "We'll go through your little nest together now that you've invited us. Me, you and my partner. Let me know if we're going to find any surprises."

"Maybe some little girl's underpants?" Misher said.

The two detectives searched the bathroom and then the bedroom. The only thing of interest to them was a bottle of Xanax.

"What's these for? Nightmares?"

"I get anxiety. They're twenty-five milligrams. The lowest dosage."

"Keep you calm to hunt the little girls?" Salerno asked.

"You're sick!" Dunmoore told him.

"I'm sick? I'm sick?" Salerno went for the music teacher, but his partner intercepted him.

"Look here, Stewart," Misher said, "My partner thinks you killed that little girl. Her name was Heather. He found the body. And there are the others," he added. "Why don't you tell us about it?"

Dunmoore paled. "You'll have to leave," he told them. "I'm going to have an anxiety attack."

"Leave? Leave?" Salerno's face was red with anger. "We'll leave when we're good and ready. You let us in and you let us look around, so you waived all your rights. We'll leave when we're good and ready! We'll leave after we've looked in your living room and in your kitchen and in your freezer and in your car, and up your fucking ass if we want to!"

Dunmoore sat down dejectedly on his small pink sofa. Salerno and Misher spent more than two hours in the townhouse and in the laundry room that he shared with his neighbors on either side. The tightly curled Afro hair in the lint trap of the dryer interested Chick.

"You getting some tender, dark meat?"

Stewart Charles didn't understand him. "She left her hair in your dryer," Chick went on. "Your little girlfriend is 'AA'-African American?"

"My next door neighbor is married to a black man."

"That makes me want to puke."

"It's the millennium," Salerno answered him. "And I bet she has a huge ass." He turned to his partner. "Chick, make sure our friend stays calm while I look around."

In a few minutes he held up a piece of picture wire. "What have we here?" he asked. "You like to tie them up, Stewart? Is that your thing?"

He bagged the wire even though there was nothing about ligature marks on the new dead girl or Heather. Chick looked at his partner, knowing it was the Kocinzki case Salerno was talking about.

The detectives took Dunmoore's toothbrush, the cake of soap from his shower and his appointment book.

With the police gone, Stewart Charles Dunmoore sat alone, listening to the old music in his head, and singing along with in his odd, sweet voice. Then he got up and sat down at the piano. That was his stage and the keys were access to the meaning of his life. He played a sad song as he thought of the children who had received the gift of music from him, sitting together on the piano bench on the flowered cushion his mother had long ago made for him.

After the search, Salerno dropped his partner back at the station. "I'll log this stuff in tomorrow," he said. "I'm going to go hit some balls."

"Sure, partner," Chick told him.

Jimmy drove to the range again and ordered a bucket. Seagulls had started flying onto the driving range and settling on the berm three hundred yards out. There was a standing offer of a hundred bucks for anyone who could nail one of them. Salerno hit shot after shot. They didn't even move. "I wonder who's dumber, me or them birds?" he asked himself.

6

Whenever he could, Inspector Zinn waited until after the shifts changed before he went home. That way, he could take a look at the personnel going off and the ones coming in. He wanted to see their faces, who was going strong and who was getting fried one way or another. He also regularly went downstairs to talk to the Desk Sergeant. At least twice a week he attended a roll call for one of the shifts of patrolmen that went out.

That afternoon, Joe Zinn was leaving his office a few minutes early. They were going to his daughter's for dinner and bringing a pork roast. The phone rang. It was the Medical Examiner.

"I got some preliminary results for you, Joe."Nessel was talking with his mouth full.

"Sure, Sam, sure. But swallow or something. It's hard to hear you through your lunch or whatever. Sounds like you got a mouth full of mud."

"You don't expect me to eat meat, Joe, do you?"

Zinn thought about the pork and sauerkraut he'd soon be enjoying. "What's up, Sam?"

"Your detective was in. My impressions are preliminary, but I figured you'd appreciate a verbal, even if it's not my final necropsy."

38

"I appreciate it, Sam. What do you got?"

"There is bruising on the arm and at the neck, but the actual cause of death looks to be pneumonia. Both lungs were filled with fluid."

"Caused by what? The Inspector asked. "We got a public health issue here?"

"Etiology unknown. I got a rush from the labs. They didn't show anything."

Zinn could hear the medical examiner light a cigarette. "What about her face, Sam?"

"You got to check with Toolmarks, but they're definitely bites, Joe, like I said. Most likely dogs. Somebody forget to feed Fido."

Even after all these years, the M.E.'s comments still annoyed him, but Zinn told him only, "Write it up."

Sam Nessel thought about saying that of course he'd write it up and that he'd have to send one copy to Homicide North, one to the district commander, one to the Chief of Detectives, and one to the police lab supervisor, but he figured why bother. He took a double hit of menthol smoke and said goodbye.

As the Inspector drove out Henry Avenue, he went over the information Nessel had given him. There was now the strong possibility that this dump job was somebody trying to dispose of their own parental neglect. That would be a relief. The Feds were a pain in the ass anyway, but Agent-in-Charge Robert Epps was a viper.

Traffic moved smoothly until the Inspector came to Dorsett Street. The bakery was two blocks down in the 7900 block, but there was a bottleneck up ahead. Zinn thought about pulling up on the shoulder, but he remembered to do what his doc had told him. He put on the radio and listened to WPEN until traffic thinned out: Bing Crosby, Vaughn Monroe. There even was a Johnnie Ray song, "The Little White Cloud That Cried". He'd tell Mary about that when he got home.

Stan Prelutsky had just been transferred from the Arson Division and was in no good mood when his only daughter brought the dark man home to meet her parents. "Zinni the Guinea" was the nickname Joe carried then, and he looked the part. Mary made it a point to introduce him to her parents with his family name and not just the one his father had been given when he landed at Ellis Island, "Mom, Dad, this is Joe Zinn. 'Zinnolkowski'," she added before her father could frown. "He just got out of the Army, and he wants to be a policeman."

Mary's mother sighed with relief, and her father nodded. Mary and Joe got married a year later and lived on the third floor of the Prelutsky's stucco twin for three years while Joe saved enough money to put a down payment on their first house two blocks away. Now, Joe and Mary Zinn had two kids of their own. Joe Jr. had gone into the service and was married and living in Portland. Elizabeth had married Tom Schmaulke, who like his father and two uncles, was with the Fire Department.

Once a week, the kids came over or Joe and Mary went over there, usually bringing dinner when they did. Since Tom hurt his neck and was out on disability, Mary made sure they did the visiting and either brought too much food or slipped her daughter some cash before she left. Usually, the Zinn's stayed for a good while after dinner was done, particularly if there was a ball game for the men to watch.

The pork roast was delicious. The smell of the pie in the oven drifted into the small, round dining room. "Smells like peach pie to me," Joe Zinn said as he walked into the kitchen.

"With chocolate ice cream, Daddy" his daughter told him.

The rest of the evening was as good as the pie until Tom's neck started bothering him. Then he started in on the black militant faction in the Fire Department. When his language got bad, it was a signal for the Zinn's to go

When they got out to the car, Joe saw two dark figures coming down the street. The Inspector was carrying his off-duty Beretta .25 that they had given him after he left the Twenty-Sixth District. He relaxed when he saw it was two seniors out for their evening walk.

The ride home was pleasant. Mary washed the dishes she had brought home from her daughter's while Joe read the paper and looked at the mail. It was a nice evening until the phone rang.

As Rook drove north on the New Jersey Turnpike, he noticed a dark blue Cadillac keeping pace with him in the center lane. The car made no attempts to hide its presence, and when Rook pulled into the rest area to cool the engine, the Caddy followed him.

He parked and moved the Smith and Wesson .45 from the console to his coat pocket. Leaving his cane in the car, he went into the turnpike restaurant to empty his bladder and drink bad coffee.

The car that had been shadowing him was in clear view when Rook came out of the rest stop. There were two men. He studied their appearance with a quick glance. They had expensive suits and blank faces, the two who had met him at Harry Raimondo's.

Rook rolled down the window of his brother's car. "Tell Carlo I'll be fine," he said.

One of them started to say something, but stopped. They both lit cigarettes and accompanied him for the rest of his trip.

Rook didn't like the shadow following him and thought about doing something about it. He exited the Holland Tunnel, and when they turned off, he drove uptown for two blocks and then west to Tenth Avenue, around behind The Saint Claire to the old warehouse building on Gansevort Street. He flashed his lights in front of the rear bay door which quickly opened.

Sid Rosen was reading *A Scanner Darkly* with his hat and coat on. "When I'm done reading this, it's yours. Your good fortune I'm allergic to books when they get old." He put the book down. "How did she run?"

Kirk was the brother who had known about cars. The Avanti was his, and Lucas felt good and bad that someone else was keeping it up. "She ran fine, Sidney."

"I'll put her away until next time."

Rook nodded. He walked out the front of the warehouse and down the block, coming up to his hotel from the opposite direction. There was no sign of the tail.

The doorman was new. "Good evening," he announced, touching the brim of his top hat.

"Tony out sick?" Rook asked.

"You mean Eddie? He fell and breaked his ankle playing street hockey with his kid. I'm his brother-in-law from over at the Essex. I'm on day work, but they asked me so I came over, the holidays coming around and all."

Rook nodded and went in. Leo was the combination concierge/night manager. He was an angular man who spit when he spoke. "There was a hand delivery for you, Mr. Rook. It came a few minutes ago. Would you sign for it, please?"

He took the envelope and went across the small lobby, half expecting to see his two new friends from the Cadillac. He counted out the cash and would deposit it in the bank the next day. There was no telling where the money was coming from and he was scrupulous about paying taxes, no reason to give anybody something to hang him with.

Rook had been offered a number of jobs after the NYPD. The investigation and departmental hearing into his handling of Kirk's killers, not only cleared him, but made him a hero for awhile.

There were two particularly lucrative opportunities. One as a director of security for a pharmacy chain and another for a retired stock broker, who made millions of dollars and dozens of enemies. Rook passed on them and an offer to do commercials for an alarm company, and went away.

He spent time in New Orleans, Chicago, and L.A. before coming back. His apartment was still there, protected by the post World War II institution of rent control. He had his disability and pension and his tastes were modest, his only interest that he had started collecting memorabilia from T.V. westerns.

His brother's murder still haunted him. Rook tried Departmental counseling, psychotherapy and even hypnotism. As a last resort he tried to buy the house they grew up in.

Only when he started doing investigations, first for an insurance company and then on his own, did he start feeling better. Maybe it was somehow being a cop again or the extra money, or just being busy, but it brought him around.

The deep disturbance from his twin brother's death receded but it did not disappear. That feeling of loss no longer hollowed him out, but that image remained, still chilling him, calling him. Reminding Lucas Rook that there was something terribly wrong that had to be made right.

7

There were three apartments on the tenth floor of the Hotel Saint Claire. One was occupied only part of the year when its residents were not in Florida, where they went to keep warm and die. A retired orthodontist lived in the second and collected serving spoons and butterflies.

Rook's living space was dark. There were recessed lights throughout, but he had not replaced the bulbs when they went out. Two standing lamps went on from the wall switch, and he clicked them on with his cane. He had two mirrors in the living room which allowed him to see into the open bedroom and his study. The bathroom was closed as he had left it. Rook made his routine walk through the apartment before he settled down.

He checked his messages. There was a call from Catherine Wren, who told him that she would not be coming to New York for the weekend, and a call from Carlo to confirm that he had received the retainer.

It was quarter to ten, not too late to call Jack O'Meara. He wanted to talk to Jack, who was a Philly detective. They had worked a case together when Rook was still with the NYPD, trying to find the runaway daughter of a New York State senator. O'Meara had found her whoring on South Broad Street.

They hooked up again the following year. Jack and his wife, Carolyn, had two rowdy boys, who had gotten themselves in serious trouble after an Eagles-Giants game. They had badly beaten a Pace College student. Rook was the detective-in-charge and got the case when four of the uniforms on the stadium detail brought the boys in. The bigger son, Sean, had the presence of mind to make it known that his father was a detective in Philadelphia. Rook gave the kids a break.

He had to work it through their mother. Jack wanted them to spend a couple of nights in the system, but that was all wrong.

It was the last time that Rook and Jack O'Meara had any contact. Carolyn called him once to say that the boy, Sean, was dead. He'd run into a retaining wall. His blood alcohol level was twice the legal limit. That was ten years ago.

As far as Rook knew, Jack was still on the job, and Rook wanted his help. Carolyn answered his call. She was crying.

"Carolyn, it's Lucas Rook."

"He's gone," she said.

"Gone where, Carolyn?"

"Gone. He's left."

"What do you mean?"

"Left. He left everything-me, the house, the Department. We've been talking. He was supposed to come by tonight..."

"What happened?"

"He should be here. They wrote him up again. He was DUI. He crashed." She paused, "Like my Sean, my beautiful boy." She started crying again. "The Department made him retire. He's working for the Bridge Authority. He brings me money, but he's not here. Nobody's here. You know he had started beating on me? Did you know that, Lucas Rook?"

"Where is he, Carolyn?"

"He's supposed to be here. I made a special dinner. Now he's probably over at Doyle's, drinking. He was supposed to be here. I can't do this no more. I'm all alone."

"I'll be in town tomorrow, Carolyn. I'll stop by. Maybe I'll see Jack."

"You'll be too late, too late."

"Call somebody. You must have somebody to call, Carolyn."

"It's too late. There's nobody." Her voice drifted away.

"I'll call you back in ten minutes, Carolyn. I need to make arrangements. Don't do anything. Just count to a hundred."

Rook called Doyle's and the Bridge Authority, but could not locate Jack O'Meara. Then he called her back. "I'll be there soon. Clean the house, make it nice and clean. Then we'll find Jack."

"Please hurry."

Rook went out of his building and walked around to Sid Rothman's garage. As he came up to the two-story brick building, the bay door opened.

"Suppose I was a bad guy?" Rook asked.

"Me or the car's owner would shoot you," the mechanic answered from behind his book.

Rook drove back down the New Jersey Turnpike. He didn't want to get there late and find that Carolyn had done something stupid. He also didn't want to waste his time and spent the ride returning phone calls, including to a prospective client who was the victim of a bank swindle. Rook got off at Exit 6, connected with the Pennsylvania Turnpike to Route 1, and arrived at the O'Meara's stucco twin in an hour and a half.

Carolyn opened the door. The table had been set, but the plates had been knocked over. A cake was upside on the floor. She held a half-empty wine bottle in her hand. Rook walked by her.

"Careless of Jack to have forgotten this," Rook said. He lifted a chrome revolver with his cane.

Carolyn watched the gun rise from the table. "I thought we'd start over. Jack and me. It's our anniversary. This room used to be our special place, Jack's and mine, like Clara's Glade."

"Clara's Glade?"

"You know, in 'Lonesome Dove', where Gus and Clara used to meet."

Rook sat down. "I recall Gus being buried there."

Tears filled Carolyn's eyes. "How he loved her."

Rook walked over to her.

"I tried to get it right," Carolyn said.

"You meant to kill him?"

Carolyn took a drink of the wine. "I wanted him to stay."

"Jack doesn't scare, Carolyn."

She looked away. Rook could see the fading bruises.

"How long has this been going on?" Rook asked.

"What?"

"What shall we call it? Post-traumatic stress? Bad brain chemistry? Acting out?"

"I don't know," Carolyn replied. "He's drinking again."

"Is he still working on the Bridge? I called there."

"He's supposed to," Carolyn said. "It's his last chance. Sixteen years with the police department wiped out."

"Where is he, now?"

Carolyn lit a cigarette. 'Probably at Doyle's, Danny Doyle's. The other Doyle's won't let him in. Or if not, he's at

McClatchy's."

"I'm going to get him."

Carolyn looked up. "Don't do anything," she said. 'It's my fault."

"I'll talk to him."

"I tried that. The counselor tried. It's like Jack's fallen in a cave and can't get out."

"Jack knows I won't lie to him," he said. "I'm going to tell him not to hurt you again." Rook stood up and put the revolver in his waistband. He recalled a quote from one of the books Rosen had given him. "'Salvation joins issue with death,'" he said.

Carolyn stared at him.

"Browning," Rook told her.

"That's kind of a gun, isn't it?" she asked.

Rook turned to leave. "That, too," he said.

It was late, and Rook was tired. He knew he wouldn't find O'Meara that night. Jack was probably holed up somewhere. Catherine Wren lived near Princeton which was half the way back to New York. Rook called her from the road. It was well past midnight. "It's me," he said.

"Lucas?"

"Yes." A truck horn blew behind him.

"Where are you? Paris, Hong Kong?"

"I'm on the four lane near the Princeton Exit."

"Are you coming here, Lucas Rook?"

"If you're alone."

She said yes, then hung up and went to put on tea.

It was after 2:00 A.M. when he got to Catherine's yellow house at the end of the winding lane. They talked for more than an hour. When Lucas fell asleep in the soft chair, she covered him with a blanket.

Rook awoke during the night. The chrome revolver was not in his waistband. Anger boiled. In comfort there was danger. Then he saw the gun on the mantel across from him. He took it and joined Catherine in her warm bed.

In the morning, Catherine Wren tried to slip out of bed without waking him. But as her foot touched the floor he awoke.

"Go back to sleep," she said. "It's six o'clock. I'm going for my run."

"Come here," Rook said.

She climbed back in and she kissed him. "Let me take my run, Lucas Rook. It will only take twelve minutes."

"More than that," he replied.

"No, the run," she laughed.

Catherine Wren was tall like Rook, but she was as light as he was dark. She had long, cool legs and he admired them as she stretched out for her mile and a half. Her auburn hair was cut short, almost boyish, but that only added to her femininity. "You go back to sleep," she said. "I'll wake you when I'm back."

Rook stood up and put his arms around her. At six foot one and two hundred pounds, he was showing his age and he stood at an angle to accommodate his bad leg.

"Are you carrying anything?"

"This is Princeton, Lucas."

He looked hard at Catherine and she went and got the stun gun he had bought her.

"Promise you'll take it with you when I'm not here," he said.

50

"I promise. Or I'll take a bow and arrow or something, like that Supreme Court Judge, Schiller."

Rook watched her from the front window and then read the newspaper. When she came back from her run, he was waiting for her. They made love in the tangled sheets and after she showered, he sat in the small tub. It was the only luxury Catherine had seen Rook allow himself.

When he went into the kitchen he saw that she had a number of bowls on the counter. "We expecting Julia Childs?" he inquired.

"I hope not. She was a spy, you know," Catherine answered. "Kind of like you."

"Not me," he answered. "I'm a pharmacist."

"A pharmacist?"

"I dispense cures," he said as he cracked the eggs.

"It's a good luck day, Lucas. You've got a double yolker. Whisk them, will you, while I get the pastry cups."

Rook stared into the bowl at the twin embryos.

"*Oeufs en Cocotte à la Crème*, except without the cream, Lucas. There's soy milk in the cupboard." She began to read aloud from the cookbook, "When the egg whites begin to coagulate, spoon them out. The eggs are done when they begin to tremble slightly." She paused and walked towards him. "And I as well."

After breakfast, they read *The New York Times* as they sat on the wicker chairs in her white gazebo. The scent of lilac was around them. Rook dozed and dreamt he was racing downhill in a car that had two steering wheels.

8

Inspector Zinn took the call in the kitchen. It was John Gabrick, the Watch Commander at the Twenty-First District. "Big Red" they called him. He had been two classes behind the Inspector at the Academy and had worked under him for three years when Zinn was a robbery supervisor.

"We got a situation here, Joe. Just inside the Two-One. Henry and Barto Streets."

"I appreciate the call, Red. What do you got?"

"We got a missing kid, another little girl. About the same age as the one that you had, 'Raimondo' wasn't it?"

Zinn wondered if it was the girl that the Medical Examiner had. "How long has she been gone?"

"Just today, Joe. Not enough time yet to put it up on the board. But I got a feeling about this. I thought you'd want to know."

The Inspector had a feeling, too. "Who's catching it?"

"I'm sending Lefko out there."

"Gene, Gene, 'The Dancing Machine'. I knew him when he partnered with Jack O'Meara," Zinn said.

"Yeah, he's alright. I thought you'd want to know."

"Thanks, Red. Listen, I got to do some food shopping at the Acme."

Gabrick knew the Inspector was talking about the supermarket at the end of Barto Street, which meant he'd be out to the scene.

"If you run into Lefko, give him my regards," Gabrick said and he hung up.

Joe Zinn washed his face, changed his shirt, and took his service weapon from the lock-box under his bed. When he came downstairs, his wife knew something was wrong.

"Is it bad, Hon?" she asked.

"It might be."

"I'll make you a cup of coffee."

Joe wanted to roll, but he waited for her to pour two cups and sat there for a while.

He kissed her on the forehead. "Don't wait up."

The Inspector thought about it all as he drove to the Twenty-First. How he was not following procedure and that maybe he was rushing things. If Nessel's formal report on the girl without the nose called it a crime that would mean that he'd kept it off the board. And if Lefko's case turned out to be a homicide, they could have a serial killer to deal with.

Zinn took a deep breath and turned on the radio. "Been here before, this kind of topsy-turvy shit," he told himself. "Let's wait and see. It'll play out." He drove over to Barto Street, Lefko was just getting out of his unmarked.

Zinn pulled alongside.

"What brings you to our fair precinct, Inspector?"

"Couple of things. The wife ran out of coffee and we were low on toilet paper, Detective."

Lefko shuffled his feet. "Yeah, there goes marriage's only peaceful moments of the day."

"You got that right, Gene. What do you got?"

"Little girl's been gone overnight. It's not enough time. She's most likely at a friend's house or hiding, but the mother's gone hysterical. She already had the Fire Department out here and the sector car twice. Big Red, Gabrick, sends me here, I'm here."

"What's their name, the family?"

"Jelks. Their name is Jelks."

Zinn knew he was pushing it, but he needed more so he would know how to handle tomorrow. If there was anything here or in Nessel's report, he'd have Salerno's case up on the board before his first shift reported. "I'll come in with you, Gene, since I'm here."

Lefko was alright with that since Joe Zinn was a boss, if not his. When they got inside, the woman was walking around in circles. "The police? Are you the police?"

"I'm Detective Lefko, Mrs. Jelks," Gene answered. "This is Inspector Zinn."

There was a scratching at the sliding door that led out to the patio.

"Sandy!" called Nancy Jelks, running over. She slid the door wide open and looked outside. "Sandy!" she called, "Annie's home!"

A black Labrador came inside. Then a middle-aged woman came out of the kitchen carrying two cups of coffee. She wore her graying hair in a bun and dressed plainly. The Inspector went over to her. Lefko was trying to get information from Nancy Jelks or at least to get her to sit down.

"We're the police," Zinn said. "That's Detective Lefko. This is his case."

"I'm Rose Colanzi from next door," the woman said offering her hand. "Annie's the dog. You know, like in *Little*

Orphan Annie', only backwards. She shook her head. "Nancy's hysterical about Sandy. Would you gentlemen like some coffee?"

"How long has Sandy been gone?" Zinn asked.

"Today. I'm sure she'll be alright."

"Was the dog gone, too, Mrs. Colanzi?"

Detective Lefko heard part of the conversation. "Was the dog with your daughter, Mrs. Jelks? Did she go out looking for it?"

"We were all right here. Right here," she answered. "Me, the baby, Sandy."

"Donald's out of town," Rose added. "He shouldn't be."

"And then what happened, Mrs. Jelks?"

She didn't answer. The detective repeated the question.

"She took the baby upstairs."

"Let Nancy answer the detective, Mrs. Colanzi," Inspector Zinn said.

"I took him upstairs," Mrs. Jelks said.

"Where was the dog?" Lefko asked.

"She always sleeps upstairs when the baby does."

Suddenly, Nancy Jelks ran for the stairs. Lefko let her go.

"She's up there twenty times an hour. I tried to calm her down," Rose said.

Zinn gestured to her white shoes. "Are you a nurse, dear?"

"Oh, no," she answered. "I just answer the phone."

The Inspector stepped away so Lefko could question the neighbor. Gene learned that there was no family discord, that Donald Jelks worked for Kodak and was in Rochester, that Sandy was a normal, happy little girl, and there was a younger son. There had been no incidents in the neighborhood.

Lefko wanted to know if the house alarm was armed, but knew he wasn't going to get anything more from Mrs. Jelks right then. "Do they usually have the alarm on, Mrs. Colanzi?"

"It wasn't on when I came over. At night I know they do. In fact it went off the other night. In the day, it's hard with the kids going in and out."

"What kids?" Lefko asked.

"Sandy. The boys next door on the other side, the twins, Francis and Albert. It was their father's idea. He's a Sinatra nut."

"How old are they, Rose?"

"The twins are five. They're a handful." She wiped a spot of dust off the end table.

"Tell me about when the alarm went off."

"Mr. Jelks, did it. He opened the window in the back room and forgot the alarm was set. He called me to say what it was."

Lefko drew a star next to that in his notes. Maybe the father set the alarm off on purpose so if it went off again, nobody would think anything of it. Fathers can want to get rid of their kids. Maybe he was doing something to his daughter and she was going to tell.

"Were you at home, Mrs. Colanzi?" he asked.

Rose looked shaken. "I wish I could have been here sooner. I didn't get home until after four."

The detective motioned for Zinn that he was ready to go.

"We'll have cars looking for Sandy all night. Tell Mrs. Jelks that," the Inspector said.

Lefko walked over, "Statistically, Mrs. Colanzi, the chances are greater than not that everything will be fine. Thank you for your help. You're a good neighbor."

"I try to be," she answered. "To look after the children."

"What do you think, Gene?" Inspector Zinn asked when they got outside.

"Fifty-fifty that somebody grabbed up the kid. And if that's so, it's better than fifty-fifty that she's already dead. Could be it's one of them post-partum things, but the other kid's almost a year. I don't think it lasts that long. I read about that 'Mary Noe' case, the one that was over in Kensington. I mean I didn't work it, just followed it like that 'Yates' case in Houston." Lefko did those little dance steps. "You had one about nine months ago. That's still open?"

The Inspector nodded.

"Maybe somebody got an appetite," Lefko said. "Let me go back and write this up."

Zinn felt the detective could be right about somebody with an appetite. Being at the scene gave him that feeling. He'd get Salerno's new case posted. If he got written confirmation of natural causes from Nessel, he'd clear it. If not, or if the Jelks job turned bad, he probably would have to deal with the FBI. There was no way Assistant Special Agent in Charge Robert Epps was going to let this pass him by. One way or another he'd find the jurisdictional elements to get the Bureau front and center.

When the Inspector got home, his wife was still up.

"I'll heat something up for you," she said. "A chicken cutlet."

"I'm not hungry, Hon," he told her.

"You okay?"

"A long day," he told her. "A long day."

Donald Jelks was stupid from his third Blue Sapphire martini and it took a while for him to realize that it was ten o'clock and he had forgotten to call home.

"I cannot drink these things," he said to Ed Mahaffey, who also worked for Kodak.

"Sharon sure can," Mahaffey answered.

Sharon Nevins was on her way back from the ladies' room in her tight, red skirt. The top two buttons of her chenille blouse were open.

"God, would I like to hump her," Ed said a little too loud.

"I couldn't even find it," Jelks answered. "I'm sloshed."

"Find what, Donald?" Sharon asked as she sat down.

Jelks face turned red.

"Oh, I see." She reached under the table and rubbed his leg.

"Boing!" Mahaffey announced.

"I gotta go, people," Don told them.

Sharon smiled. "Be careful when you get up."

Jelks went out to his rental parked in front of the restaurant. The cold air started to clear his head. His hotel was only ten minutes away. Jelks was sure he could make that without an accident, but he wished he had a cup of coffee.

He made a wrong turn out of the parking lot and headed for the lake. Realizing his mistake, Donald made a U across the road and headed back to downtown Rochester. The neighborhoods went from wealthy to middle class to ghetto as he approached the hotel district. There was a closed supermarket and an old billboard advertising that the circus was coming. The gas stations were closed and their lights were out.

When he got to his hotel, Jelks went to the line of vending machines in the back of the lobby. The coffee machine was "out of order." When he got upstairs, the red message light was blinking on his phone.

Jelks looked at his watch. "She'll be pissed." He picked up the phone and retrieved the message. It was Nancy. She sounded hysterical and doped up at the same time. "Sandy's not here. Sandy's not here, " she said over and over.

He called home. His hands were shaking and got a wrong number. Jelks tried again. Nancy answered. "Come home, come home," she cried. "Sandy's gone. She's not here. Sandy's gone."

Jelk's heart dropped, and he got cold inside. He tried to get information from Nancy, but she was crying and saying it over and over again, "Sandy's gone, Sandy's gone."

"The baby? The baby okay?" he asked.

"Come home. Come home."

"Is Stevie okay?"

"Sandy's gone. She's gone."

"I'll be right there." Then he realized he couldn't be. "Can you call your sister?"

"Joanie's not here."

He hesitated. "Did you call the police?"

She didn't answer, and he could hear her crying away from the phone. Donald called to her, but she didn't answer. He hung up and dialed Rose Colanzi. The call woke her, but she agreed to go back over and stay with Nancy until he got home. She told him that the police had been there and that they said it was too soon to worry.

Don Jelks called the airlines. There was nothing he could do until six in the morning. He thought about driving, but that wouldn't get him home much earlier and he was in no condition to make it.

He booked an emergency seat on the US Air first flight out and drank himself to sleep.

9

Stewart Charles Dunmoore remarkably resembled his mother, who still played the organ on Sundays at the United Methodist Church in Shinston, West Virginia. Stewart had her wide hips and most strikingly, her auburn hair, which he had worn long since high school in the mistaken hope that he could transform his years at the piano into some kind of popularity.

But even as an eight-year old, the length of Stewart's fingers made people stare. He often dreamt that those fingers had a life of their own, wriggling and then going off in different directions. When he was not at the piano, Stewart kept his hands balled up or hidden away in his pockets. He was ashamed of them and worse, that somehow they were responsible for the miscarriage of the little brother or sister that his mother carried and he wished were never born.

His father had wide hands which he used for years to make television sets for the now defunct Dumont Corporation. Bernadette Dumoore's hands were graceful and she encouraged her son to sit next to her as she moved them up and down the piano keys.

On Sundays, Stewart sat with his father in church, and watched her play the organ. From time to time, his father sang along during the hymns, but just as often as not, he drifted off into a snoring sleep. Stewart learned to gently nudge this man who smelled of cigarettes and whose black hair tufted out of his ears and the collar of his Sunday shirt.

Stewart tried for his father's affection by playing ball and learning how to use tools, but he failed at these things as he failed at school. His attempts at joining one of the high school cliques or even making friends amongst the few geeks did not succeed and he succumbed to the derision of his strange appearance: his round hips, the copious amounts of his auburn body hair and his long hands. Years later he still heard it inside his head, "Tang-tang-the-orangutang."

In his senior year, Dunmoore wanted to have a party at his house where the piano would be his salvation, but by then his father had gone mad. They said it was a delayed reaction to fighting in the War, as well as losing his job at the Dumont plant. Bill Dunmoore sat and watched the TV set with the picture off and MIGS and ZEROES flying out.

When her husband got like that, Bernadette Dunmoore would take Stewart upstairs to her room. "Play for me, dear," she would say as they sat on the corner of her bed and his fingers played imaginary keys on her night stand. She hummed along to "Clair de Lune" and made wistful ringlets in his hair.

It was during one of those magical duets, Stewart's playing and her softly singing "Claire de Lune," that William Dunmoore, her husband of forty years, shot himself in their living room rather than surrender to the yellow horde.

The police had first come for Stewart when Heather Raimondo was found dead by the side of the road. The two detectives had hit him, pushed him down. The square, dark one had ground his face on the rug-covered stool where Heather Raimondo had put her feet. They had called all the parents of his students. Detective Salerno had come back twice in the middle of the night.

It was after the police had let him alone, that Stewart Charles Dunmoore packed all his piano books and his lesson plans and his music, his CDs and his carefully wrapped collection of 78's. He put them in the back of his car and drove away. He drove all night to his mother's house and rang the bell until she woke up.

Bernadette's auburn hair had turned to gray, and she had become hard of hearing. But she took him in and held his hand, and as the morning came into her little home, Stewart played "Claire de Lune" for just the two of them.

10

He awoke without an alarm. He had been doing that for as long as he could remember, even when there were two of them, his twin brother sleeping in the bunk bed below him, or later in the twin bed across from him.

Rook readied for the Raimondo assignment, checking the Glock he would bring and his .38 police special. He packed his weapons, a loc-pic set, and a half dozen plastic tie hand cuffs. Rook put the fentanyl into his shaving kit. The sedative was inside a standard 3 mg "Epi-Pen" epinephrine auto injector, easily explainable as an emergency antidote for severe allergies. Lastly, he changed the .45 cartridge in his cane.

Then he sat at the kitchen table, stretched out his bad leg, and reviewed the information that he had. Rook had confirmed that Harry and Carlo Raimondo were what they appeared to be. The union lawyer was a mob wanna-be.

The kidnaping and murder of Heather had made grisly headlines for a few weeks and then moved off the front page and faded away. There was some discussion of a suspect which went nowhere. Jack O'Meara could help with that.

The lead detective in the Raimondo case was James Salerno, who had twenty-three years on the force. The profile in the *Daily News* revealed that Salerno was married with two children and had been an All-Catholic linebacker at Monsignor Bonner High School. He had been in the Ashau Valley with the First Calvary and received a bronze star and two purple hearts. The pictures showed a dark, square man with angry eyes.

The newspapers presented two theories: one, that Heather was killed by someone close to the family; and the other, that a passerby had killed the little girl. There was one clumsy attempt to draw in the Jon Benet Ramsey case, which allowed three day's copy. The signature photo of the case was haunting— Heather Raimondo holding a bouquet of flowers in one hand and waving goodbye with the other.

Rook called over to Sid Rosen's garage to see if his Crown Victoria was ready. It was the prototypical law enforcement car and perfect for this job. Rosen told him he was finishing the oil change and that the Ford would be ready in a half hour as he wanted to wash it down. Rook asked him to put on a Pennsylvania license plate and bring the car around when he was done. Then he called around until he found Jack O'Meara.

"Who wants him?"

"An old friend from the NYPD, Jack."

O'Meara recognized the voice but didn't want anything to do with Lucas Rook. 'I'll tell him when I see him."

"A thousand dollars," Rook said.

There was a pause. "What do you want, Rook?"

"It's police work, Jack."

He poured himself a drink. "I'm on retirement."

"If you still got the chops, it's private."

"I got no license."

"You can work on mine, Jack. It's a week's work. You interested?"

"No funny stuff, Rook. And I ain't working across no active police cases." O'Meara took a Lucky out of his shirt pocket and fired up. "How'd you find me?"

"That's my business."

"Which is exactly what?"

"Finding the bad guys, Jack. I'll pay a thousand dollars, and maybe you can do a good deed."

"Fuck the good deed, Rook," O'Meara spoke through an exhale of the licorice smoke. "I want it in cash and up front."

"I thought you were a good idea, Jack, but I can call somebody else."

"Okay, okay, but one-third up front. And expenses."

Rook could hear the tap of a bottle on the lip of a glass.

"Don't push it, Jack." We'll talk about it over a bottle of Jim Beam."

"I don't do nothing off-color. I got my pension to protect."

"It's detective work. I'll be down tomorrow. You pick the place."

O'Meara needed the money. He took another drink. "How about you call me when you get here. Bring half. We can meet at the Airport Sheraton."

"Three hundred."

Jack knew that would have to be good enough. "Right," he said. "But one thing, Rook."

"What's that? Jack?"

"Don't be calling my house no more."

"No need, Jack."

Rook brought two bags. He carried one over his left shoulder and one in his left hand as he walked around to Rosen's garage. Sid was waiting for him outside, leaning against the Crown Victoria.

"You look good, Sid. So does the Crown Vic."

"You need anything done while you're gone?"

"I'm good to go. Maybe look around for a four-wheel for me. Something for foul weather, riding up people's steps."

Rosen nodded and handed him a bag. "Two Joseph Conrad paperbacks, to keep you company," he said.

Rook drove back down the New Jersey Turnpike to Philadelphia, half expecting some of Carlo Raimondo's union boys to be following him again. He often had that kind of feeling that he was waiting for someone to join him.

Joe Zinn arrived back at his precinct as one of the wagons from the overnight shift was pulling in. He could only see a driver, and there were supposed to be two uniforms in the vehicle.

Instead of parking in his spot on the ramp, the Inspector parked near the van and walked over. Officer Mackrel knew there was no way out of talking to the boss and that would certainly include a conversation about his absent partner.

"A good shift, John Mackrel?"

"The usual, Inspector," he answered opening his door. "We played ambulance all night. Caught one bad call. A domestic. My partner threw his back out. It was our last job."

"He should file an injury report, especially if he's saying IOD."

"He's got the heating pad on it. He'll be in next tour."

"He should fill out the form, John."

The officer nodded. Zinn went back to his car. He knew

66

that Mackrel was probably lying to protect his partner, and that maybe that was a good thing—unless he was protecting somebody with a drinking or gambling problem.

The Inspector drove up the ramp and parked in his reserved spot. He went in the side door and up the fire stairs. Two cops were on the steps. They tried to hide their smokes as he went by.

Zinn stopped at the Watch Commander's office. The room served all three shifts. Skip Buechner was still there, waiting for the second shift commander to come in so they could brief each other. This was a long standing practice initiated by Zinn, and it worked well except when somebody was late.

"It's a good morning, Joe," Buechner said.

"It is, Skip. We have a peaceful shift?"

"Number Two wagon caught a bad one. An MVA. 'Tyronne' was all smoked up. Got a mother and a baby. She was driving a Chevette. It looks like no car seat for the kid. Bad all around."

"Mackrel tells me his partner threw his back out."

"His wife's got lymphoma. The bad kind. She's getting chemo. They got two kids. He used up all his leave. We'll probably see him 'Injured On Duty' sooner or later." The Watch offered a stick of gum, but Joe waved him off.

"Talk to him, Skip. I sympathize, but I don't want our people misusing their leave. It throws our numbers all off."

"Will do, Joe."

"Any 'crimes against the person' overnight, 211's or 233's?" Zinn asked.

Buechner looked at his sheet. "We had a bump and snatch up 'on the border,' but we'll get him. I want to use the decoy."

"Good idea"

"You want paperwork on that, Inspector, or just send him out?" The Watch Commander took another stick of blackjack gum.

"Write it up, Skip. What's your count on 201's the last week? I don't want to wait for the monthlies."

Buechner didn't know what Zinn wanted, whether he was wanting to know what was going on in the street or whether he was checking up to see he wasn't playing the numbers game. He hesitated. "I'll have to get back to you, boss."

The Inspector knew what that meant. His precinct, like all others, was understaffed and overworked and it was a time-honored practice to dispose of cases and raise the clearance rate by downgrading the crimes from serious ones like rape to "investigation of person."

"I'm not asking if you're downgrading or 'unfounding complaints'."

"Joe?"

"Call me when you get the reports pulled for me, Skip."

"No problem, Inspector. By-the-by, we picked up Caruso again. He's back on the street a week and he tries another liquor store. We grab him up, and he starts in with that voice of his again. The uniform said he stopped traffic with the singing."

"I heard him once," the Inspector said. "He started right in his holding cell over at the 10th. There wasn't a dry eye in the house when he was done."

Zinn went in to his office. John Gabrick would be home from his night shift at the Twenty-First. He called to see if there was any word on the missing girl, "Eileen, it's Joe Zinn."

"Hi, Joe. How's Mary? I'll get him for you," she said with the Brooklyn accent she had never managed to get rid of.

"The Jelks' girl is still missing, Joe," Big Red told him.

The Inspector thanked him and went to see Sam Nessel. The Medical Examiner's office was across town. Zinn drove there without calling. He made better time than he thought. Then he realized it was too early. There was a decent diner on the way. He stopped for coffee and a bran muffin, which he ate at the counter while he read the newspaper.

He arrived just at nine. The receptionist, an extraordinarily large woman, wearing lots of beads, was doing a crossword puzzle.

"Inspector Zinn for Sam Nessel."

She continued with her puzzle book.

"I am waiting. I'm standing here."

"I am on break," she replied without looking up. "I get one morning break and one afternoon break. You're disturbing my private time and my workers' rights."

The Inspector walked by her.

"You can't do that!"

"You're not here," Joe answered. "You're on break."

He walked down the hall and over to the M.E.'s office. There was another receptionist sitting there.

"You're not on break, are you?" Zinn asked.

"I'm back now," the lady with the seventies' hair-do answered. "We stagger them. That's our union rep's idea." She gestured to the large woman doing the crossword puzzle. "That way someone's always ready to serve the public."

"I'm grateful for that. Tell Sam that Inspector Zinn is here."

"I'd be glad to do that, but Dr. Nessel is not in."

"Where is he?" the Inspector asked.

"I'm sure he's home. Dr. Nessel is out ill today."

"Oh?"

"He called in sick this morning."

Zinn walked back out the way he came. The first receptionist was still doing her crossword puzzle. Zinn had the feeling that the M.E. wasn't sick at all and drove out to see him.

Sam Nessel maintained a nice stone home outside the city in the Delaware County suburb of Broomall. His ability to maintain a suburban residence and a City job derived from the fact that his position as Medical Examiner had been "grandfathered" in. This was a practice that the Inspector very much disapproved of. He believed that public servants, particularly those in law enforcement, should live with the people they served.

Nessel's home was identical to the two adjacent to it. None of the three homes in the cul-de-sac had house numbers. However, there was Sam's Cadillac parked in the first driveway with the City of Philadelphia's "Official Business" sign in the rear window.

Inspector Zinn walked up the faux cobblestone path and rang the bell. There was no answer, but a dog barked at the front window.

He rang the bell again. When there still was no answer, Zinn walked around to the rear. There was a yard where the dog should have been, the Inspector thought, rather than jumping on the furniture inside. Adjacent to the back yard was a detached garage. The Inspector could see a light on and could hear machine noise.

As he walked over to the garage, the back door opened and the dog ran out. A tall, thin woman was at the back door. The Inspector recognized her as Virginia Nessel. They had met at the Policemen's Ball and at one or two other functions.

"Can I help you?" she asked.

"Your husband's expecting me. I was admiring your dog, Virginia. What's he, a poodle? One of those mountain dogs? Sam in the garage?"

It was too much information for her to handle all at once. 'He's a Bouvier."

"Like Jackie Kennedy?"

She didn't get his joke but then she recognized him. "Inspector Zinn, isn't it?" she asked. "I'll call Sam from the house. He can't hear anything on the outside when he's in there working. Would you like a cup of coffee?"

"No, that's alright. I just need a minute."

As she went into the house to call her husband, the Inspector slipped a credit card into the garage door jam. He entered just as the phone rang. Nessel had his back to the door. He had an autopsy saw in his hand. The saw was running. as was an overhead exhaust fan. The M.E. was wearing a white mask and was working at a low table.

The phone rang and rang until Zinn went over and turned off the exhaust. "She's going to tell you I'm here for our meeting, Sam," the Inspector said.

Nessel turned with the saw still whirring in his hand. Joe Zinn reflexedly reached for his .38. He was surprised that he had done that and disguised the movement as though he was smoothing out his jacket.

Nessel removed his mask. "Joe," he said, "what are you doing here? What's up?"

"They told me you were sick, Sam."

"You know the way it is, Joe. Sick leave-use it or lose it."

Zinn walked over to the workbench.

"It's my hobby, Joe." He displayed a long piece of maple in which he had carved shapes of angels.

"What's with all the little girls, Sam?"

"They're angels," Nessel told him. Then he realized what the Inspector had said. He was angry. "Yeah, Joe, you're right. I only thought these angels were moulding for my granddaughter's nursery." Sam Nessel turned the exhaust fan back on and lit a cigarette.

"You shouldn't smoke with all these solvents and thinners around."

"I shouldn't smoke at all, probably but then again my growth is already stunted, right?" The Medical Examiner paused and took a double hit on his menthol cigarette. He took another drag and dropped the butt on the floor. "You got something you want to talk to me about, Inspector?"

Zinn stared at him. "I still have questions about our dead little girl, a dead little angel you could say."

The work table electric switch was regular height and Sam had to reach up to it.

"You want to know if I made a mistake? I make lots of them," he answered. "How many livers do you want me to tell you about? Little girls' livers I cut out and weigh after I chart the temps. That's how I determine the time of death. You know that, don't you? Do you know how many livers I handle every day?" He lit another cigarette.

The Inspector let Sam Nessel go on.

"You want me to say I made a mistake on that girl with the missing nose, Inspector Zinn? That she's a murdered child?

I make mistakes all the time. You know how many corpses I touch a day, a week, a year? Some years there's thousands. I make lots of mistakes. I got my protocol and I follow it. I follow my protocol when I cut out their livers and saw off the tops of their heads. And you know what, Joe?" he said as he blew out a smoke ring. "Not one of my patients complains."

"You done, Sam? When you're done, you can tell me what you got to tell me."

"Like what? Maybe you want to know if the same maniac that killed Heather Raimondo murdered somebody else? I can't tell you that. Only that the girl without her button nose was dying anyway." He crushed his cigarette. "I do the best I can, Joe."

"I'm sure you do, Sam. I'd like to go over your official findings on that little girl."

"You can read my report when I file it. Goodbye, Joe." The Medical Examiner turned his saw back on and began shaping the wings of the wooden angels with his stubby hands.

11

Rook checked into the Embassy Suites off Route 291 near the Airport. The four-story facility catered to the business man with a need for an extended stay. The parking lot was spread out like a fan and off to the right was a small swimming pool covered with a black tarp and layers of dead leaves. The location was good, reasonably close to the Raimondo crime scene and Interstate 95 to Center City.

He parked in the back, checked in, and went to the top floor. His room was in view of the elevator. The fire stairs were off to the right.

After acquainting himself with the room, Rook unpacked his weapons and set up his work station on the twin bed closest to the door. He thought about his new assignment as he skimmed one of the books Rosen had given him.

Rook's experience as a gold shield detective and his years "for hire" since the murder of his brother, had taught him that, as often as not, logic got you nowhere. While he gathered as much information as he could, he always followed his instincts and he always started in two different directions.

He checked-out the Airport Sheraton bar and then drove over to Salerno's precinct. The drive down from New York was hard on the old injury, but he left his cane in the car and walked slowly to hide his limp.

Desk Sergeant Joe Garrett, a huge black man with a square head, did not receive him warmly.

"NYPD." Rook held up his old badge.

"What?" Garrett asked without looking up from his newspaper.

Rook put away his shield. "I'd like to talk with your Commander."

"What?"

"Your Commander, Inspector Zinn."

"About what?"

"It's personal."

"About what?"

Garrett made a big show of folding up his paper. "You're tiring me out, my friend."

"What are you bustin' my balls for, Sergeant? You can call upstairs like I'm giving you the courtesy to do or I can call Inspector Zinn at home late tonight and tell him it's thanks to you."

Sergeant Garrett decided it wasn't worth the risk. He offered the clipboard. "Sign your name and put your shield number. For Purpose of Visit, put Administrative." He saw Zinn go out the side door in his sweat pants and running shoes. "The Inspector will be back in about an hour."

Rook knew that circumventing Zinn would get him lots of trouble later, but it would be worth the shot if he could talk to Salerno now. "Jim Salerno on the shift?"

The Desk Sergeant put his square hand on the clipboard. "You didn't ask about him. You got something personal with him too?"

"Just wanted to buy him a cup of coffee. If it's like anything we got, yours tastes like shit. There's a Dunkin' Donuts I passed. You want something?"

"Bagel and cream cheese would be good. Two. Black, three sugars."

Rook went back out. He sat at the counter and had a cup of coffee and a donut with three Advils for his throbbing leg. A woman cop came in, cupping her cigarette like a stevedore.

He ordered Garrett's coffee and bagels and a dozen assorted donuts in two separate bags. Rook carried them all in his left hand as he entered the station house. He gestured with one of the white bags. "One of the many benefits of the job."

"Should swear off the snacks, but a big man got to eat." Garrett held his hand out for the bagels. "You going upstairs you got to check your weapon with me. Rules and regulations, Detective. You're from another jurisdiction, you got to check your weapon."

Rook removed his Glock from his hip where he was wearing it police-style, rather than in the back as he had become accustomed to. He dropped the clip, racked the slide, and showed the empty breech. "You want me to sign in again, Sergeant?" he asked.

"You're good." Garrett took the .45 and pointed to the door on his left with his bagel. "Up a flight and to the right. The Inspector's not back yet. You can wait in the coffee room."

Rook went through the door and up the stairs carrying the bags of donuts. The building smelled like cops. Familiar sounds. He missed it.

The coffee room was the third room down the hall. The door was off its hinges. Two detectives were inside playing cards. Rook knew from the newspaper photos he had seen that neither of them was Salerno. He put the white bag of donuts down. "Compliments of NYPD."

"You know Andy Sipowicz?" the one with the pink face asked.

"Don't mind him," the other said. "He's just tired of losing." He wore a striped shirt and bow tie.

Rook walked over to the hot plate and the two percolators. "Ain't we all," he said.

"I heard that," the one with the bow tie said. Then he added, "Gin!"

"Shit!" the pink-faced cop replied. He was a wiry man with red hair and freckles. He pushed his folding chair back, almost toppling it. "Our coffee tastes like shit. Yours any better?"

"Nope," Rook answered. "Administration got its own espresso machine though."

"It figures," the detective said. "I'm Brian Muldoon. My partner here, who just won for the first time in his life, is Sal Raddichio."

"My partner, Brian, here, is going to law school at night which is where he's learning to cheat."

'Kiss my flat Irish ass," Muldoon told his partner. "What brings you to 'the City of Brotherly Love'?"

"Looking for a bad guy."

"Ain't we all," Raddichio answered. "Anybody we know?"

"Nope. I just wanted to pay my respects to the Inspector. I'm way off the board here," Rook told them.

"On what?"

"It's old and closed. One of Salerno's. He in the house?"

"I haven't seen him," Raddichio said.

Rook caught the change on Raddichio's face. The detective was understandably suspicious of any interference and protected his own.

"We're going to save the world," Muldoon said. He left with his partner and the donuts.

Rook waited for another half hour before Joe Zinn came in. The Inspector was under six foot and thin, but he was full of energy and confidence. Zinn extended his hand. "What can I do for you?" he asked.

"Lucas Rook, NYPD homicide, retired. I'm here to pay my respects and learn your ground rules."

"You the brother of the twin—eight-ten years ago? I remember that case. They ever clear that?"

"It got cleared."

"You're not on the job anymore, as I recall."

"I'm working private. Licensed in New York. If it goes anywhere, I'll hook up with somebody local. You have any preferences?"

Inspector Zinn looked away. He felt for the man in front of him because his brother was killed in the line of duty, but that went only so far. "Who you working for?"

"I was hired by the parents of Heather Raimondo. I know this is your territory and it was your case. I respect that."

Zinn straightened the clock on his desk. "I don't allow any outside influences to disturb my house, Rook."

"Anything I get I turn over to Detective Salerno. I'd like to have a sit down with him."

"Salerno won't talk to you unless I tell him to. And, as I see it, you only can disturb my people and my precinct." He gestured to the doorway.

Rook made no motion to leave. "I'm going to get you a baby killer, Inspector."

"I don't like interference and I don't like surprises."

"Salerno?"

"He won't like you any more than I do."

12

Rook arrived at the Airport Sheraton bar fifteen minutes early, but Jack O'Meara was already on his second Dewars and water. O'Meara gestured to the bartender as he walked up. "Run the tab for me and my uncle here. He's real generous."

"Thoughtful of you, Jack. Let's take a table. We can watch the airplanes."

O'Meara had grown beyond thick. He was combing the hair over his bald spot and his skin was blotchy. "What's up with the cane, Lucas?" he asked. "I heard you got it pretty good, but I didn't know you had gone crippled."

Rook sat down. "Still the charmer, Jack. And still in shape."

O'Meara finished his scotch and water. "I can move pretty quick when I got to. You about to make me temporarily rich, Rook?"

The waiter came over. He was a tall, thin man with a prodigious nose. His walk and gestures were effeminate.

"Dewars and water," O'Meara said. "And don't put your thumb in my glass."

Rook looked at the waiter's name plate. "Give me a Miller Lite, will you, Bill."

"Certainly." The waiter put cocktail napkins in front of each of them and a silver plated bowl of mixed nuts in the front of Rook.

When the waiter left, Rook gave his answer, "You'll get rich, Jack. For awhile anyway."

Jack picked through the bowl for almonds. "I'm all ears."

"Don't hurt your wife again."

O'Meara leaned across the table. His breath was foul. "You done? Now shut your hole if we're doing to do business."

Rook took a sheaf of twenties from his inside pocket. "I want you to do some good old-fashioned police work."

"Who for?"

"I'm working for Harry Raimondo."

"The union guy? Used to break kneecaps before he blimped up. Somebody killed his kid, right? A little girl?" He moved on to hunt for cashews.

"I work for him. You'll work for me."

"You got workers' compensation, Rook? And a 401K?" O'Meara waved for the waiter.

"Yeah, Jack, and your own secretary to give you a hand job every day at noon."

"The case is open, closed, what? No way I'm fucking up my pension"

"I already met with Joe Zinn." Rook took a sip of his beer. "The case isn't cleared, but it's on the back shelf. It was Jimmy Salerno's case. You worked with him, right?"

"Eight years. If he couldn't clear it, nobody can. He's a bulldog. He's got no forget in him. And he's stand-up. When I had my trouble with the Department, he could've hurt me, but he didn't."

"I want you to do is talk to him, Jack. See what he got. You can tell him that the case is still his."

"He might if I told him it was my job, me working for fat Harry Raimondo."

"Tell him that, Jack."

The drinks came. The waiter smiled at Rook as he left.

"Somebody's in love, Rook," Jack snickered.

"I pay you a third now and a third when Salerno gives you anything that's not newpaper stuff. I give you the last piece when you get a sit-down with me and Salerno."

"He won't go for that."

Rook knew that O'Meara was making himself indispensable.

"You could charm the whiskers off a rat, Jack. Tell him I'm working for you, whatever."

"What about we grab the murdering fuck up, Rook? What about the back end?"

"I do the grabbing up. I get him, you get the fourth third."

"I got somebody in mind. You give me a piece of the fourth third upfront, I give you the name now."

Rook picked up the menu.

"You give me the extra three hundred now, otherwise I forget the name altogether."

Rook peeled off some more twenties. "Here's one, Jack."

"Name's 'Ralphie Cheese.' He's the deli man over at Foxes. Likes little girls."

O'Meara finished his drink. "We grab up the baby killer, maybe I get reinstated, you let me call it in to Jimmy or whatever."

"I'll think about it. Have another Dewars on me."

Jack waved his thick arm. "Oh, Mary, a double, please."

Rook drove over to the playground where the little girl had been snatched. He had told Raimondo to meet him there. He wanted to see the big man's face while they walked the scene.

There were two sets of swings, one for the little ones with little chairs and safety bars and one set for the older kids. A jungle gym with rubber padding around it was off to the left and there was a fort made out of red and yellow plastic pipes. To the right was a blue-painted cinder block building and on the other side of that was a basketball court.

The blue windowless building housed two restrooms secured by hasp and lock. A door marked "office" was likewise locked. He would check with the City Recreation Department whether the rooms were open the day that Heather Raimondo got grabbed.

The ground to the basketball court was uneven with gullies cut in by the rain and bad landscaping. Rook wished he had brought his cane. The fractures to his kneecaps and tibias were almost a decade old, but the instability was lasting.

A basketball game was running full court with another five waiting for the winners. Others sat around to watch the play. Some of them were drinking from quarts of malt liquor inside of paper bags. The smell of marijuana wafted up. Rook pinned his gold shield to his outside pocket to announce his presence, but no one paid attention or even hesitated in passing around the joint.

As Rook stood on the sidelines, a big, red-haired kid swatted a jump shot out of bounds. The ball bounced over and Rook deftly took it on the bounce.

"Ball!" called the afro'd black who missed the shot.

"It's mine now," Rook told them.

"Yo, yo, yo," said another player. Soon a gang of them was walking towards Rook. He took out his .45.

"You crazy?" afro asked.

"You gonna shoot somebody?" said the redhead.

"Worse," answered Rook. "I'm gonna kill your ball."

"You what?"

"I'm going to put a .45 caliber, copper jacketed, hollow point through this Spalding 'A I' model. And then I'm going to come back every day you're running ball, and I'm going to do it again. I'm going to do it every day until I'm satisfied."

"Then fuck yourself," one of them said.

Rook smiled "I'm going to count to three, and then I'm going to throw this bad boy up and put a round through it."

"What you need?" the leader of the group asked. He wore a bright blue bandana on his head pirate style.

"I'm looking for the fucking creep that snatched up a little girl from this playground and then killed her, threw her body by the side of the road."

"We don't do that shit," the pirate said.

"Didn't say you did. Your ransom price is to tell me about any creep or freak you've seen around here."

"Including you?" a round one with a goatee asked.

"I'll be back tomorrow," Rook told them. He holstered his weapon and launched a long shot at the basket.

Harry Raimondo parked his Lincoln across from the playground to meet Rook at the swings as they had agreed. The Great Dane was in the back seat, getting agitated at the

84

prospect of going for a walk. The car rocked as Raimondo negotiated the exit of his massive girth.

Rook waited for the two of them to get out. The dog must have weighed more than a hundred and fifty pounds and was pulling hard, but the big man was surprisingly agile and kept the dog on a short leash.

"This is Sebastian, Rook."

"We met at your home that night with your brother, Carlo, and that lawyer."

"Right, right."

"You wanna walk with me, Harry. Maybe you'll remember something."

"Sure, sure."

They walked around the swings and over to the red and yellow plastic fort, then to the blue concrete building. They walked this route a couple of times and then over to the stand of trees at the horizon and back. Harry was quiet and Rook left him that way.

When their trip wound up back at the swings, Rook looked at Raimondo. "Remember anything?"

Harry leaned against the chain-link fence and gestured over to the swings, lines of tears running down his big face. He brushed at them with the back of his hand. "Ain't it something," he said. "My little girl used to swing on them things. Happy as a lark, going back and forth."

The dog was standing up against him. He patted the dog's head. "It's called 'the lean', Mr. Rook. Danes do that. I used to bring Sebastian down here with Heather. He used to bark at them swings."

A maroon Jeep pulled up and parked in a spot across from the entrance to the playground.

"That's Atkins, the black guy I told you about."

"From the Fire Department," Rook said.

"He'll have his boy with him. I guess you want to talk to him now."

"I'll say hello, Harry."

The fireman got out of his car with his son and stood against the door until traffic passed. He was tall, almost six four, and wore a Green Bay Packer's jacket. His skin was the color of cedar and he wore his hair closely cropped.

As Atkins crossed the street, he saw Raimondo and waved, but walked up the block to the next entrance.

"He don't like dogs. The coloreds don't, you know. Hey, Atkins," he yelled. "I want youse to meet somebody." Raimondo walked away from the entrance so the fireman could come in. The boy was wearing a Donovan McNabb jersey and carried a football. Rook walked up to them.

"Mr. Atkins, I'm working for Mr. and Mrs. Raimondo for awhile." Rook handed over his business card with the emblem of the chess piece. "I was a police detective before I got this," Rook gestured with his cane.

"Injured on Duty?"

"It's a long story. The Raimondo's got a bad story."

"I heard that," Atkins said. He sent his son to play in the fort.

"I got to help them finish it. Which is why I'd like to talk to you. I know you probably talked to the other detectives and you need this like a hole in the head, but it won't take long."

"That's alright. It could have been my boy. Could we talk now though. My boy won't be in the way."

Rook questioned him at length. The fireman added nothing.

Harry walked back to his car, rolling like a ship with each step. He let his dog into the back seat where he had spread out a bed sheet.

"I could bring you to my house and back. There's room," he told Rook.

"I'll follow you." Rook started over to his vehicle.

"Sebastian's good in the car."

"That's okay, Harry. I'll follow you."

"I'm going to make a stop. You like Italian pastry? They make good rigot pie. I got to stop for gas also."

Rook followed Raimondo and pulled into the gas station when he did. The fat man got out of the car by swinging both feet and grabbing the outside of the car's roof with his left hand. When Harry stood up, his pants slid below his waist and his shirt rode up. Rook could see the wooden handle of a revolver.

Harry went inside the gas station and came out with a handful of Slim Jims. He pulled the plastic wrappers off two of them and passed them to this dog who took them gently. Then he called, "Put in twenty. It's paid for."

Rook was familiar with the way back to the Raimondo home, but not the route Harry was taking. He accelerated at every light and turned corners without signaling, but Rook stayed with him.

When Harry pulled into "Mastrangelo's" small parking lot, Rook waited across the street. The only other parking spot in front of the bakery was occupied by a blue Bronco.

Two men came out of a deli next to the bakery as Raimondo went in. The Great Dane stood up in the back seat as much as he could and began to bark furiously.

One of the men got in his Bronco while the passenger waited for him to pull it out. As was his habit for years, Rook memorized the men's appearance and the vehicle's license plate number.

The dog was still barking when Harry came out carrying two white boxes. He kicked the passenger's door. "Sit down!" he screamed. "Sit down!" Soon he was back on the main road, and in ten minutes they were at his house.

Raimondo pulled all the way forward in his driveway and let the dog into the fenced yard behind the house. Rook parked behind him, leaving enough room to turn across the lawn to get to the street.

Harry walked back from his car. "You've been here before," he said. They walked the peony-lined path in single file to the side door. An alarm beeped as he entered his house. The fat man punched in the code.

"I'm home," he called. "She's probably upstairs. You want some espresso? Otherwise, I'm making just coffee."

Raimondo put the cake boxes on the table and gestured to Rook to take a seat. "You want a shot?"

"I'm good."

"You sure?"

"I'm sure. I'm working, Harry. Coffee's good."

"Right," the big man said. He put one ricotta pie on a glass plate and the other one in the refrigerator.

"You want to see the house, you said. Eat some rigot. Have a coffee. Maybe the wife will be up then. She sleeps a lot."

Rook took note of the kitchen. It had all the latest appliances and a bay window that looked out onto the square fenced yard. There were the matching maple table and chairs with yellow cushioned seats and a set of yellow canisters for flour, sugar, and salt. Magnets on the refrigerator and two drawings, one of a little house with huge flowers in front of it and one of the Raimondo's holding hands labeled "My Family."

He wondered what was in the drawers and closets. There was always one drawer with odds and ends, old keys, photos, match books.

The dining room was off to the left. Down the hall and to the right was the "parlor" as they called the sitting room. A piano dominated the parlor.

"Heather take lessons?"

"Yeah. He came here. His name's on the frig. He teaches a bunch of the kids. His name is Steward, I think. I'll get it for you." But Raimondo sat there and looked out the window. "You want to walk around, Mr. Rook. I'll show you," he said after awhile.

"I'm alright, Harry. I just want to walk around. I'll be taking some notes." Rook copied the list of phone numbers from the bulletin board: the pediatrician, the music teacher, Raimondo's work and celphone numbers. There was an advertisement for Argente's Tumblearama.

"Did Heather do gymnastics?"

"That's my sister-in-law's place. We thought about it. Maybe next year." Then Raimondo realized what he said and shook his head. "You want to look around? Go ahead."

Rook went through the downstairs. The dining room had flowered wallpaper. There were candlesticks on the mantle and a pair of China angels. The table had a crocheted cloth on it, and all of the chairs were pushed in. The only things in the breakfront were tablecloths and napkins.

The parlor barely held the piano and two matching striped chairs side by side with their backs to the window. Rook looked through the music lesson books. They were marked with comments, "Start here," "Good." Some of the pages had gold stars and some had colorful stickers. The handwriting was flowery.

There was a wicker basket near the front door. It was overflowing with mail and magazines. Rook looked at the cable and phone bills and two from credit card companies. He copied the return addresses from some envelopes and checked the magazines.

When he went back to the kitchen, Raimondo was pouring himself a second scotch. The dog was under the table.

Harry's shoes were off and Rook noticed how small his feet were.

"I'd like to see her room," Rook said.

The dog followed them, but stopped halfway.

"He won't come upstairs. He's a nice boy. Let me go up and close the wife's door."

Harry climbed the stairs with difficulty. Rook followed. The carpeting went up the steps and down the hall. Harry closed the door on the left and opened the one on the right. It was a little girl's room with a canopied bed. Mrs. Raimondo was curled on it, asleep.

Rook and Raimondo went back down the pink stairs. "Things are falling apart. " Harry lit a cigarette. "I ain't smoked in twenty years before all this."

The dog trotted down the hall with his head lowered and lay on his mat in the kitchen.

"Something else is fucked up, the way the dog got that guilty look." Harry walked back to the steps and then to the parlor. "God damn it," he yelled, and Rook could hear the crashing as the big man threw the bench up on the piano. "This ain't right, Rook," he said when he came back down the hall. "My dog peed on the piano, the bench. He never does that. Christ! The whole place is falling apart! When is it going to end?"

Rook went from his client's to the public library. Without access to the local police files, it was the best place to do his spadework. He checked the newspaper archives going back ten years.

There were two similar cases, but that went nowhere. The killer in both was a neighborhood teen who shot himself with his father's gun. "Not too phallic," Rook said out loud.

He paid the modest computer fee and went into a half-dozen chat rooms until he found the one he wanted, the local nest of child fuckers. There was a lot of code talk, but no uncovered identities.

Rook went up to the periodical room to clear his head. There were New York papers there and he caught up with the ongoing saga of the World Trade Center mess.

13

It had been a rotten day for Detective Salerno. Mired in paperwork and then finding they had calculated his sick leave wrong. He was on hold with Benefits, trying to straighten out his hours when he got it from the Assistant District Attorney, "You were not prepared at yesterday's preliminary hearing, Detective."

"I'd testified five hundred times when you were still standing in front of the mirror pretending you were Diana Ross."

"That's going to get you written up," the ADA said.

Jimmy hung up on her and when the sick leave clerk disconnected him, he dropped the phone into the wastebasket.

The Inspector called him into his office. Zinn wanted Rook around so he'd have a firewall to put between his Department and the FBI. If the vic in Nessel's refrigerator or the Jelks girl turned out to be homicides, ASAC Robert Epps would have college boys all over the place.

"I wanted to talk to you before I went out, Jimmy."

"This a sitting down or standing up meeting, boss?"

"There's a P.I. in from New York to work on the Raimondo case."

"You want me to run him off?" Salerno asked.

"The guy was on the job. Gold shield. His twin brother, too. The bad guys took him out in front of that restaurant in New York eight or nine years ago."

Jimmy stood up. "He's an outsider, boss. He's going to fuck up everything, contaminate it all."

"Keep your pressure and your voice down."

Salerno stared at him. "What's my blood pressure got to do with it?"

"Raimondo is still your case. I'm only asking that you don't mess with Rook if he stays inside procedure."

"You saying I don't do my job?"

"I did not say that, Detective." The Inspector took a deep breath. "Let's get back to the subject, my subject. I'm asking that you don't blow a gasket about Rook."

"Right, boss. Maybe this is not our house any more. Maybe we let anybody run our cases."

"He'll be here a week, Jimmy."

Salerno ate some Tums. "It's not right, Joe."

"He knows my rules and to stay out of our way. And anything that he gets is yours. We got an agreement."

Salerno shook his head. "Right, an 'agreement'."

"The guy gets a week. He was a gold shield detective until they blew his brother away. I hear he squared it himself. He's alright."

"Who's he working for, Joe?"

"He's working for the Raimondo's."

Jimmy crunched another antacid. "Christ, he's probably mobbed up."

"He's straight. I checked with Manhattan South."

Salerno started for the door. "I'm taking a week. I'm not going to be here while he fucks it all up."

"I need you to stay around, Jimmy. Just stay around."

Salerno slammed the door on his way out and went back to the squad. "Anybody seen Chick?"

"In front of the mirror," somebody answered. "Coordinating his ensemble."

Esposito came by on her way to see the Inspector. "Your partner's in Interrogation One."

Salerno headed down the hall. As he turned the corridor, he could hear the distinctive baritone voice of their operatic felon, Caruso, singing from *Porgy and Bess*. Jimmy went in without knocking.

Chick Misher and two other detectives were sitting at a gray metal table.

"Crazy, huh, pardner?" Chick said. "Some crooning we got here."

"You don't know the half of it. You want to go hit a bucket?"

Raddichio held up his finger "Shush," he said. "We got art here."

Caruso shifted into some light opera from *The Desert Song*.

"Mario Lanza here did robbery, and assault. What do you think, Jimmy? Should we get our perp here a record contract or '302' him?" Misher asked.

Caruso stopped on account of their crosstalk. The two detectives walked out. "You could commit me the way my day's going."

"Your day gets worse, partner," Chick answered, "because the driving range is closed. They're resurfacing the parking lot. You want to try and get nine holes in, you could try the course. I got to meet with ADA Hattie Williams about one of my cases going to be called tomorrow."

"That too, Chick. I just hung up on her." Salerno put on his coat. "Sometimes I think the whole world needs to be involuntarily committed. I'm going to get a couple of holes in before it gets too dark."

The bordering trees were turning gray as Detective Jimmy Salerno walked down the fairway. He could hear voices up ahead. Two old men were sitting in the descending dark. One of them had a flashlight on a stick.

"What are you doing?" he asked.

"Who wants to know?"

"The Philadelphia Police Department wants to know."

"I don't see no badge," the other one said. He wore stained painter's pants and a long black overcoat.

Salerno walked over. He carried a five-iron in one hand and was reaching for his slapjack with the other.

"I'm Maguire," the one with the hat told him. "This here's Malone. He's my partner."

"Partner at what?" the detective asked. "You guys up here playing hide the pickle?"

"That ain't right," Malone said, "to be talking to us that way."

Salerno noticed the canvas bag over his shoulder. "What's in the bag, gents." He held out his hand for it.

"It ain't nothing," Maguire told him.

"You let me be the judge of that." The detective took the bag. It was heavier than he thought. Inside were about three dozen golf balls.

"We come up here twice a week. They buy them off of us at the pro shop, There's a big barrel there. They lose them, we find them, me and my partner, Malone. They hit them and lose them again. It's coffee money."

Jimmy walked away and teed up one of the balls from his pocket. He hit it hard, but he did not hit it straight.

"You opening up too soon," Malone said.

Salerno gave him a dirty look and teed up another ball. He sliced his next shot too.

"You guys flap your mouths once more, I'm going to run you in."

"For what?" Maguire asked. "We ain't done nothing wrong."

Salerno grabbed the bag from him and dumped it out. "Receiving stolen goods. Now get out of here before I run you in."

Malone started to say something back, but Maguire took him by the arm, "C'mon partner. They'll all be in the rough anyway. We'll get them in the morning." They used their light to make their way across the course and through the trees to the row houses on the other side.

It was night then, but the detective's eyes had gotten used to it. Jimmy hit all of the balls he had dumped out and the six other ones that he had brought. Those that made it up the fairway, he hit again. Then Salerno walked off the course and back through the woods.

When he got to his car, he could see the left front tire was flat. "Shit!" he said ringing the hubcap with his five iron. "This day's been a perfect piece of shit."

Salerno changed his flat tire by the light of the overhead street lamp. The tread looked good, but the valve cap was gone. He figured the two scavengers he had just run off had done it. He made a pass through the neighborhood for them, but came up empty.

As it was almost eight-thirty, Jimmy called home. He got the answering machine, and then he realized it was the second Wednesday of the month which meant his wife was at her sister's.

"I'm going to Higgins', he told the machine. "Get myself a crab cake sandwich. I'll bring you something if his desserts look good."

A spot opened up close to the front door of Higgins' bar as Jimmy was pulling into the parking lot. When Salerno walked inside, he saw his partner sitting next to the side window. Jack O'Meara was at the bar downing a cold draft.

"It's old home week," Big Bill Higgins called.

"I'll drink to that," Jack answered.

"Draw me a cold one, Bill," Salerno said. "The world's dirty. I got to wash up."

"You got that right, Jimmy." Chick gestured to O'Meara. There was no love lost between Misher and O'Meara. A thing between the two of them eight years back cost Chick "time in grade" and he never forgot Jack not backing him up on a brutality charge.

"You alright, partner?"

"Flat tire," Jimmy answered. "And I shanked a hundred tee shots."

Jack O'Meara lifted his glass to Salerno as he walked by to the men's room. When Jimmy came out, O'Meara offered to buy him a drink.

"Going to eat with my partner." Salerno answered.

O'Meara had work to do for Lucas Rook. He followed Jimmy to his booth."Let me buy you two a drink, for old times."

Misher held up his coffee cup. "You're not invited, O'Meara."

Salerno tried to steer his partner away from trouble.

"The stew was good. You got any more stew, Bill?" he called across the room.

"The stew is good," Higgins answered. "I'll send some over."

"I had some," O'Meara offered. "Like it was homemade."

"With a vodka chaser?"

O'Meara started back at Misher, but Salerno cut him off. "Give Jack here a slice of your coconut custard pie at the counter, Bill."

Chick ignored the uninvited guest. "They 302'd Caruso."

O'Meara persisted in his attempts to be included. "He still around?" Jack asked. "I had him in twice in '90. Drove me nearly crazy myself. Six hours of show tunes."

Misher leaned across the table. "That what did it, Jack?"

"Fuck you, Chick. You still got a hard on."

Big Bill came over with a bowl of stew in one hand and a piece of pie in the other. He pointed to his sign—"It's Us Against Them," he said.

"Right, Bill, right," Chick said. "You got any more of them little onions?"

"So, you're working the Bridge, Jack?" Higgins asked

"It pays the bills," O'Meara said. "How about a pitcher, will ya? Three glasses."

Misher had enough. "I gotta be going. See you tomorrow, partner. Don't take any wooden bridge tokens, Jack."

Jimmy Salerno slid his plate over so that he could see out the window. "How ya been, Jack?" he asked. "How's Carolyn?"

"She never got over our boy dying." He finished his beer and poured another. "How's by you, Jimmy?"

"Getting fat and rich, Jack."

"I heard that. What's doing at the house? Joe Zinn handling the world?"

"Yeah, he's alright. I guess you can't ask more than that."

"Nobody bats a hundred percent, Jimmy."

Salerno looked at him. "You mean a thousand percent, Jack. A hundred is one out of ten. The animals'll take over behind those numbers."

"What'd I say?"

"You said a hundred percent. Like in school."

O"Meara nodded. "My job's okay, Jimmy. No glamour, but every day's got a clean slate. No bad cases around, you know what I mean?"

That was enough for Salerno to know he was fishing. He got up to take a piss.

When he got back to the table, Misher was standing there. He motioned his partner to step away so O'Meara couldn't hear. "Jimmy, the boss got me. Says your beeper isn't on."

Salerno used Higgins' phone behind the bar. When he came back to the table, his fists were clenched and his face was flushed.

"Fucking piece of shit," he said putting a ten down for his bill and the tip.

"What's up, partner?" Misher asked. "You look like you're going to explode."

"They found another dead kid."

"I'll roll with you," Chick told him.

O'Meara heard them and went up to the bar. He was filled with self-pity that he was off the job. But he was glad that he wouldn't be trying any more to pry info from a brother cop, even if it would cost him Rook's money. The case was alive again on account of there being another dead kid and that meant he was out.

"You look kind of twisted up, Jack," the bartender said.

"I guess I am, Bill. It's all that important work on the Bridge. And, besides, I just lost five hundred bucks. Dewars and water, Bill. A pair of them."

14

Joe Zinn was getting a haircut in his kitchen when he got the call from Downtown. "They found another little girl, Joe. On Forbidden Drive, just inside the park. It's not yours, probably the Nine-Two's but you get the job. We'll take care of the details, but as of an hour ago we need a Task Force and it's yours. Keep us informed."

Zinn walked over to the sink to shake out the towel he wore around his neck.

"I got to go."

"There's a little piece that's uneven I'd like to get for you, Joe," his wife said. "That piece above your ear."

The Inspector called Salerno, "We got us a situation, Jimmy. I got a call from Downtown. There's another dead kid. I'm putting together a Task Force. I want you to head it up. It's up to you whether Misher's in."

"He's my partner, boss."

"The job's at Forbidden Drive. Take charge at the scene. I'm going back into the house."

When Salerno arrived, he could see a perimeter had already been set up. Yellow barricades closed the entrance to the park. There was a blue and white, an unmarked, and the Medical Examiner's wagon was around the bend on the right side of the road.

He pulled over to the left and walked over. A rookie waved him off. Salerno hung his gold shield from the front pocket of his coat. "I ain't no school teacher , son. Who's the ranking?"

"My sergeant." The patrolman motioned to the squad car.

Sgt. Hosner was an ugly man, who feigned intelligence by wearing his glasses on his nose. He recognized Salerno. "You're a little outside of your neighborhood, aren't you?"

"This job's being tasked over to me, Hosner."

The sergeant adjusted his glasses. "Lucky you. You got paperwork, I'm happy to turn this piece of crap job over to you."

"Paperwork is in the pipeline, Hosner. What you got?"

"The vic's a little girl. We got her tagged and bagged. Lefko tells me it's the Jelk's kid from the picture he seen at the house."

"Crime Scene been here and gone?" Misher asked.

Hosner put his clipboard down. "Crime Scene didn't show. The vic's already in decomp. The little one's go pretty quick."

"You stupid fuck!" Salerno told him. "You fucked up."

"Kiss my ass, detective. The scene's good. Nobody contaminated nothing. They told me to secure. I did that. No way I was going to let the body go to the rats or whatever. Forensics doesn't show. I'm not going to wait forever. The scene's good. You got a problem, you write it up or you and me can take a walk."

"Anytime, you piece of crap," Jimmy told him. "Now why don't you go home before you get yourself hurt."

Hosner hacked up a ball of phlegm and spat out the window. Then he adjusted his glasses and drove away.

Salerno walked over to the unmarked. It was empty, but the two detectives were standing nearby. He recognized the one leaning against the tree as Gene Lefko. He didn't know the other, a thick chested man with a graying crew cut. They were arguing about whether or not canned goods were bad for you.

"Can't you taste the metal, Fitzy? It's like lead or something."

"Maybe with pineapples if you leave them in the frig."

Lefko started to say something about tomatoes, but saw Salerno. "James," he acknowledged. "Welcome to another slice of hell."

Fitzgerald switched the cigarette to his left hand and held out his. "Dan Fitzgerald."

Salerno didn't take it. "You fucked up my crime scene, gents," he said. "You couldn't wait for forensics to get here."

"Bullshit, this is bullshit. You know this guy, Gene?"

"Jimmy Salerno," Lefko answered.

"This is tasked over. I'm going to need your statements." Fitzgerald turned away.

"And your clothes…" Salerno said.

Fitzy turned back, squaring himself the way cops do to make themselves look bigger than they are. "This is fucked. You don't got rank on me or nothing and I don't see where you got any authority here anyways. Let's go back to the house, Gene."

Lefko started to say something, but Salerno cut him off, "Both of you, your spoor is all over the place. You fuck up again and I'm personally going to see you get jammed up."

Salerno's celphone rang as Fitzgerald and Lefko started for their car. It was Inspector Zinn. They spoke for moments before Salerno called out, "Gene, your new boss wants to talk to you."

Lefko came over. He was not happy to hear that it was Inspector Zinn and that he had been tasked over to work with Salerno and Misher, but he made the best of it. "I identified the vic, Inspector. Sandy Jelks. I'm on the scene."

"All over the scene," Zinn told him, "from what I hear."

"C'mon, Inspector. We got the call. We're told to secure the scene. We do. The M.E. shows. Crime Scene doesn't. 'Get the scene secured' is what my lieutenant tells me. That's what we do. The vic is bagged. The leaves she was found in are bagged..."

"You want me to call Captain Dordick? Nate should be home right now enjoying supper. He'd like that. Or can you wait for the paperwork, detective?"

Lefko shuffled his feet, the way that got him his nickname. "I got..." he started, but the Inspector had already hung up.

"Gene, Gene, the Dancing Machine" Salerno said. "It's because you did such a fine job here. You want to ride back in with your partner and pull you own unit off the board, that's fine, but you got to be back in an hour."

Lefko nodded and went to his unmarked.

"And I'm serious about those clothes. Both of you bag them up," Salerno told them.

Fitzy gave him the finger as he drove away.

Misher was talking to the cop up at the barricade when he saw the Feds pull up. "Give me your flashlight," he told the uniform. Chick signaled down to Jimmy and then went to meet them. A tall black man in a banker's suit was getting out of an immaculate sedan, followed by Assistant Special Agent in Charge, Robert Epps. Misher could tell him by his fiery red hair. Chick shined the flashlight on the ASAC and waggled it back and forth so Salerno could tell that they had company. Then he shined it directly on the big agent.

"You redirect that light, Detective," Renaldo Dellum said, "or we're going to have a situation here."

Chick wasn't afraid of him, but didn't want to tangle with Epps over it. He pointed the beam at Dellum's shoes. "My, you got a good shine," he said. "They teach you that Quantico or you buff those wingtips yourself?"

"I was at Cornell Law School while you were glomming free lunches in your polyester," the agent answered.

"Ratchet it down, Renaldo," Epps said. He smoothed the lock of red hair back off his forehead. "Listen, Detective," he told Misher, "we can do this the easy way or the hard way. You can let us through right now so that we can begin working this case, or you can play chicken with the United States Government and find yourself walking midnight foot patrol for the rest of your life."

Salerno had seen the his partner's signal and went over to the Medical Examiner's van. "Go back in, now!" he told the driver. "Tell Doc Nessel not to do nothing until he hears from my Inspector."

"I don't work for you." The driver didn't look up from his auto racing magazine.

Salerno grabbed him. "You get your wagon out of here right now or I'm going to put you so far into the system that it'll take a safari to get you out."

"Your point is made," he answered. "But when I get back in, I'm going to file a grievance."

"That's fine. You do that. And while you're at it, you can file one on the little girl you're carrying around in a rubber bag."

When the M.E.'s wagon pulled away, Jimmy walked up to meet his partner and the Feebs. "What brings you out on this lovely evening?" he asked.

Epps recognized him from a bank robbery job they worked two years ago. "Salerno, isn't it? This case is ours now. Check with your boss. If he hasn't been so directed yet, he'll hear through channels in the A.M."

"Then this is ours until then because I've heard nothing. And there's nothing 'federal' about this anyhow."

"This scene is ours with or without your cooperation," Dellum said.

The ASAC cut him off. "I'll be looking at this job and other ones. And maybe we'll have a look at your crime reporting while we're at it. That will make a lot of folks stand up and notice now, won't it, Detective?"

"Is that a threat there, Bob?" Misher asked.

Epps straightened his maroon and gold tie. "You're busting my balls, but I appreciate your territoriality. Your people can secure the scene until our special units get up here. Abduction and Serial Killers will be here at 'oh nine hundred.' In the meantime, my people will be taking the victim back in for our forensics."

The ASAC looked at his watch, letting the expensive timepiece linger so the locals could see it. "Dellum, get your people here. I have a late dinner meeting."

The detectives did not respond.

"The victim," Dellum repeated. "We'll be taking the victim back in."

"I can't help you there," Salerno answered. "The DOA's out of my hands."

"That's bullshit," Epps said, starting back from his vehicle. "As sensitive as you people are about your crime numbers, you didn't lose a case here, did you boys? Tell your boss, my people will be in his office in three hours with a writ."

"We'll have coffee on." Misher watched the Feds drive off.

Salerno chewed some Tums. "Let's go get the vic, partner," he said. "I want to get the physical evidence before it's all fucked up."

They drove after the Medical Examiner's van with their grille lights on and the bubble flashing on their roof. As they drove away from Forbidden Drive, Salerno watched the way they lit up the woods.

15

Rook waited for Catherine Wren in Rittenhouse Square. Art students sat and smoked. Apartment dwellers waited with little plastic bags for their dogs to make a mess. There were two drunks, one of them in a fine suit, and a pair of pick-pockets starting their run. Rook wished he could scoop them up and clear the park. He found an empty bench that faced the right direction.

Bonatelli's was to his right. Cherry wood tables were bolted to the pavement. Waitresses posed and waltzed in low-cut blouses and black Capri pants. A dog walker came by with his hands filled with leashes, an anchor for two pugs, a beagle, and a nervous greyhound. A pair of joggers in matching outfits passed him by. Catherine Wren came up Locust Street in a tweed suit with a slit skirt. Her fine legs showed with each step.

Rook walked to the corner to meet her. Catherine kissed him on the cheek. Do you like my new perfume?" she asked. "It's called Gardenia's in the Night."

He thought about flowers in the book of poetry that Rosen had given him, but it escaped him.

"Can we sit outside?" she asked.

"Eau de exhaust. It's my favorite scent."

"Nothing that a glass of white wine can't cure," Catherine smiled.

They sat and sipped their drinks as the traffic went by. Rook pointed to a hawk gliding down from one of the office towers to a black tree in the small park. "He's looking for an unsuspecting dog. Or a small child, perhaps."

Catherine ordered a Caesar salad and blackened red snapper. Rook had chopped steak.

"If you're trying to get me loaded, Lucas Rook, it will not be difficult. And it will not be necessary. I have a canopied bed for the two of us half a block away."

"A canopied bed?"

"Isn't it charming," she answered. "There's a bed and breakfast of all things in the center of this city, not half a block away."

Rook raised his glass. "To the canopied bed."

Two panhandlers came up. The white one wore a hooded sweatshirt. The black had construction worker's hands and one bad eye. The two of them approached the first table where a bald man sat with his wife and daughter. They were wearing mink and eating pink dessert. The bald man gave the beggars a dollar.

"You got more than that," the hooded one said. The big one moved in closer.

Rook turned in his chair. "You're done here," he told them.

They came over. "You gimme five dollars," one said. "Each," said the other.

Catherine looked for the waiter.

Rook slid his chair back a bit. "I said you're done here."

The family in their furs got up and left.

Rook cleared his jacket for his gun, but made no reach for it. "It's over," he told them. "Go away."

"Don't, Lucas," said Catherine as she went for the manager.

The one-eyed man moved in. The hooded one followed. A patrol car came around the Square as it happened. The second one had a box cutter in his hand, the razor edge held close and sly. He circled around. The big man yelled and starting coming hard.

Rook hit him across the throat with his cane and then pummeled the other onto the cherry table where the bald man had been sitting.

"He tried to kill my friend here," the white thief said as the police came up.

"That's a lie," Rook showed his New York shield.

Catherine was back and shaking.

"Pick up your friend here," the cop told the panhandler. "Find yourself a nice corner across the river."

"Would you like another table?" the manager asked. "We can seat you inside."

"We're just leaving," Catherine replied. She turned to Rook. "I'm going home," she said.

He put his hand on her shoulder, but she would have none of it.

"You frighten me," she told him.

As Catherine walked away, Rook thought about the confrontation he just had. He knew that he was right in going after those thugs. Kirk and him had seen the same kind of thing over and over again when they were on the job. They knew when the bad guys needed straightening out and they knew how to do it.

Rook went back to his car and drove away. He drove to where the little girl had been dumped by the side of the road. Someone had hung a campaign poster on the fading cross.

The mist that had hung like cigarette smoke had lifted and he walked the railway tracks. There was nothing there, no ideas. No sense impressions except the odd feeling that someone was up ahead. Perhaps a ghost. Perhaps the killer of little girls.

When Rook got back to his room, there was a frantic message waiting for him. He called Carolyn O'Meara back. Her phone rang and rang. Rook decided to drive by. This time he went across to the Roosevelt Boulevard Extension, then up to Whitaker Avenue and over. He tried Carolyn again by phone, so he could turn back around. He called Catherine, but got no answer there either.

The O'Meara's house looked different than before. The sun was down, but he could see how the front of the house was in bad repair. The black wrought iron railing across the little porch was coming loose.

Rook went up the front steps. The veneer on the shutters was coming off. There were lights on inside, but when he rang the bell, there was no response. He walked around to the back of the house. A glass pane in the storm window was cracked and sealed with tape. The back door was unlocked.

He opened the door slightly, looking for alarm contacts. There were none, so he went inside. "Carolyn, it's me. Your door was open." There was no answer.

The kitchen was clean. The rest of the downstairs was straightened-up except for the room he had seen her in before. The plates and the cake were still there. Carolyn O'Meara had put a big sheet of plastic over all of it. Rook went upstairs, but no one was there. The double bed in the front room was covered with shoes.

As he was coming back down, he heard a car pull up. Even with his bad leg, Rook moved quickly, and was out the back door in moments. He went across the yard, his walking stick making a sucking sound in the wet ground. There was a dark van parked in the driveway next door. Rook stood behind it as Jack O'Meara went up and then back down the front walk.

"She fucking changed the locks. You got a key?"

"Not hardly, Jack. I was looking for you."

"Checking on me, you mean."

"That, too."

"Well, you can ram it, Rook. You can stick your cane so far up your ass you'll bruise your tonsils. I quit. I don't want your money. So you come near my house again, I'm going to hurt you bad."

"Don't tough guy me, O'Meara. You got the wrong one for that."

Neither one of them moved.

"I'm done with you. I told you that. They got a new job come in. Another kid got snatched. Another little girl. They'll open up the Raimondo case for sure. And I'm not losing my pension, thousand dollars or not." He took a smoke from his shirt pocket. "Besides, I don't like you."

"It's not a thousand, Jack. You only owe me half of that."

"I owe you? You stoned on something?"

"You took five hundred. You gave me nothing. You give me something else or you give me back the money. Give me something, Jack, maybe I pay you the rest."

O'Meara lit up. He wasn't working with Rook any more and he wasn't giving back the money. He took a half a step to the left. "I'm done here. I gave you Ralphie Cheese. You get nothing else. No money, no nothing." And you mess with Salerno, he'll bury you."

"Jimmy had his eye on somebody for the Raimondo case. I want to know who it was."

O'Meara took a drag. "I'll give you that, Rook, for the other five. Then we're even. We all knew who it was up in the Squad, so I'm not giving you nothing that only stupid asses like you don't have. Jimmy never let go, but he never came up with nothing."

"For five hundred dollars, Jack. The answer is…"

"Fuck your humor, Rook, and fuck you, too. We're done. The guy's name was Stewart Dunmoore, the piano teacher."

"Get me what else you can, Jack. I'm going to get it anyway. I might as well be paying you instead of somebody whose still on the job."

O'Meara crushed his butt under his shoe. "Go fuck yourself." Rook smiled.

There were no messages or mail waiting for Rook at the Embassy Suites. No one had attempted entry to his room. He sat on the other bed and read the local papers. The phone rang. It was O'Meara. "Dunmoore lives alone. He has no history, writs, or warrants. His driving record is clean. He was sued once four years ago, but that was settled. No liens or judgments. You get the address when I get the dough."

"Thanks, Jack. You talk to Salerno?"

"I told you I was staying out of that. I still got friends."

"I want to talk to Salerno. I'll pay you for that."

O'Meara lit another Lucky. He liked the way the years of smoking had deepened his voice "I gave you Ralphie and Dunmoore. That's all. Pay me what you owe me or I'll come get it," O'Meara said and hung up.

Rook was glad for the information, but he questioned the motives. Usually when somebody resurfaces to a cop, they are hiding something.

He took a shower, wishing the motel had a decent tub so that he could soak his leg. They had hurt him bad before he had gotten the last of them. They had tied him up with piano wire in the back of a transmission shop and had burned him with battery acid. Then they broke his legs with an iron bar. The right one healed, but it took plates and screws to repair the four fractures in the left.

Rook was under the hot water too long, so that when he stretched out on the bed he fell asleep. He dreamt of his brother. It was if he were floating, yet somehow standing still in a mirror that moved. He was a mirror looking at a mirror. A gun was in his right hand, and there were two in the image pointing back at him. In the dream Lucas Rook held each gun like a magic wand.

The telephone awoke him. It was Carolyn O'Meara.

"Can you come by. You know, for coffee? I can't be alone now. Jack called and he was all drunk and ranting and I can't find him." She sounded desperate.

For reasons that he didn't quite understand, Rook drove over there. Carolyn had left the front door open.

There were no marks on her, but she looked worn out.

He sat down on the single chair. Carolyn handed him a drink. "Thanks for stopping by. Southern Comfort okay?" she asked. "It's the only comfort that I get."

Rook sipped his drink.

"Let me fix you something, Lucas. It'll only take a minute."

"I'm good, Carolyn."

"You sure? It's no bother."

"I'm good, Carolyn, really. Just wanted to see you're alright. Thanks for the drink."

She walked him to the door and lingered for a moment too long. Rook pretended not to notice. "Take care," he said without turning around.

He had driven by a Chinese restaurant on the way there and stopped to eat. There was a sign on the window saying that it was closed for repair. Somebody had changed the "R" to an "L."

Rook settled for a fast food place where he lingered with *The Heart of Darkness* that Rosen had given him.

16

Rook's first attempt at Ralphie Cheese came up empty, but he knew he'd grab the perv up quick. There wasn't a deli man in the world who got three days off in a row. And if Ralphie had split, he'd track him down with some help from O'Meara or the NYPD.

Fox's Deli was in the Fairmount part of the city, where real estate developers were still trying to replace the third generation blue collar families with market-makers and lesbians.

The store was three aisles wide with the slicer and the hot food in the back. Domestic ham and American cheese was good enough for Jack Fox to raise a family on, but his son, Shelly, brought in imported meats and cheeses.

Ralphie wrote stuff up on the greaseboard he didn't even know what it was. He laughed when writing up that they were selling boiled tongue. He had more than one joke to tell about that, which helped hide his hunger for little girls. That hunger, that thirst consumed him, for their hairless bodies, their unseen clefts, their wide, crying eyes.

Rook went in and bought a newspaper and a can of Dinty Moore and went to the delicatessen in the back. He fished a roll from the bin and handed it over. "Ham and cheese," he said, "mustard and a little butter."

Ralphie took the roll. He was a wiry man, whose gray hair was tightly curled. A port-wine birthmark stained his face.

"Domestic, Imported, Italian, Salt-free, Low fat, Boar's Head?" One of his hands was in a plastic glove. The other had clear polish on his nails.

"Cheese is cheese."

Not to Ralph Morris it wasn't. He had thirteen kinds and it was a creamy, sweet gift that he cut special and passed over to his special girls. Always kind enough and smart enough to ask, "Can I give the little sweetie a taste?" And always the predator to watch them take it in their tender lips.

"We got a dozen kinds, neighbor. We got domestic, low-fat, Alpine Lace, Goats, Monteray Jack, Colby, French, Greek, Jewish, Gourmet. You name it and claim it. I slice it and price it."

"Ralphie Cheese right?"

"Some of the moms call me that." He slathered the roll with mustard and ran a row of shredded lettuce and pre-sliced tomatoes. After wrapping the sandwich and marking the price with a grease pen, he passed it over to Rook.

"Anything else? And please use the tongs. I'm supposed to say that to all my customers." He looked at his watch, "Lunch crowd should be starting now."

A nurse came in and an old man in a Sunday suit. Then three secretaries and a dark haired girl about ten with a hand-written list.

Rook walked around the store so that he could see Ralphie's face when the little girl came to the head of the line. "Hi there, strawberry shortcake," the deli man said. "Did you go to church on Sunday?"

She didn't understand.

"Next time you go, take some 'holy cheese'." He handed her a piece of Swiss with his ungloved hand.

Rook saw Ralphie's face turn, if only for a moment. He had seen it before. Motherfuckers who rubbed baby oil on little boys until they loved it. Always thinking they were doing right, somehow blessing the life they were cursing. Ralphie Cheese passed a slice of the Swiss between his gold-capped teeth.

The store closed at nine. There was a sign that said the deli closed at eight. An hour to clean up. The owners would let Ralphie close up only if they took the cash with them.

Rook threw the sandwich in the trash and drove away. He came back at a quarter to eight to watch the door.

At five after nine, Ralphie Cheese came out in a leather coat and walked around the corner to his six year old white Caddy. The car was neat and clean, with a blanket in the back.

Rook was up against him close as he was opening the door. "Ralphie, boy," he said, "You forgot to ask me about the mustard. Yellow, brown, seeded, Grey Poupon, whatever."

The deli man turned to see him, remembering him from the morning. "I don'…"

"I heard you like little girls."

Ralph Morris had lived his fetid life for too long to take chances. "Sure I like kids. Don't everbody?"

"No, no Ralphie, the other way. They're so sweet ain't they, friend? So smooth they are. Like chocolate covered butter creams, the hand-dipped kind."

Ralphie Cheese had a hard-on, but more than that, the deep-in feeling of fear and power and the trembling expectation of it all.

Rook went on, "They think it's dirty, but it's just the opposite, so sweet, like buttercream."

The deli man turned around.

"I got something for you," Rook said. "Pictures first and then the sweet buttercream if you want. You got a place to talk? Back inside, maybe?"

There were only two lights on in the store, one up front over the registers and one from the changing room. "We can go in there," Ralphie said. "Let me see."

Rook followed him to the back. "Sweet, sweet buttercream," he said.

The changing room had hooks along the walls and two benches. There was a bin for them to leave their dirty aprons.

"Jack O'Meara sent me." Rook watched the cheese man change to a wary predator.

Rook brought his blackjack out fast and hard and whapped him on the clavicle. Ralphie bellowed as the collarbone snapped and his right arm dropped to useless.

"Jack tells me you like to use those naughty girls."

"No, no," Ralph Morris said, "Not like that." He had a folding knife that he carried and he reached for it.

Rook had seen evil a thousand times before and brought the spring loaded weight down again. Ralphie slumped on to one of the benches.

"Heather Raimondo. You dumped her by the side of the road."

"I don't…"

"About eight months back. Pretty little girl. You snatched her from the playground. Then you killed her, Ralphie boy."

"No, no. It couldn't be."

"A head shot with this thing's going to turn your brain to oatmeal, cheeseman."

"No, no. It couldn't be. I was away. For the thing, the thing I do. O'Meara sent me away. I just got out three months ago."

"I guess Jack holds a grudge," Rook said. "The Irish are like that. Particularly Irish cops." He turned to go. "But I guess he had his reasons." Rook jacked Ralph Morris across the face, shattering his jaw.

The cheeseman's mouth filled with blood. Rook grabbed him by the back of his collar and dragged him to the hamper. "You're making quite a mess," he said as he knocked him into the dirty clothes.

While Salerno and Misher sped after the little girl in the black rubber bag, Rook went after Dunmoore. The most recent phone book had Dunmoore's address in both the residential and music instruction sections. While there was no way that the piano teacher would be that easy to find, it was enough for Rook to start his spadework.

Dunmoore's home address was in a semi-circle of garden-style townhouses with patches of grass on each end. In the middle of the semi-circle there was a monument of sorts with a light fixture on top.

Rook drove around the complex, but could see neither Dunmoore nor any activity in the townhouse. As he swung around in front, a blue Subaru hatchback pulled up. The driver was a tall black man in a green coat. The passenger was a heavy white woman wearing a green hat. Their vehicle was loaded with groceries. As the two of them got out to unload their bags, Rook walked up to Dunmoore's unit, carrying an envelope with him.

"I'm sure he's not in." She put down her groceries while her husband unlocked their red front door. "We're his neighbors."

"I've got a check for him, for my daughter's piano lesson." He talked on so she would. "We were away so it's late and I wanted to bring it over to him personally. We certainly don't want to lose our spot. We've already missed one lesson."

"I could hold it for him," she said. "We're bringing in his newspapers and any of the mail that doesn't go through the slot. It's odd not hearing the piano. He's been gone for a couple of days. Didn't tell us he was going. Isn't that right, Ozzie? He just did. I guess it was family business, huh Ozzie?"

"I hope he hasn't moved," Rook said. "He's so good with…"

The husband came back inside and picked up one of the bags. "We let the papers pile up and we're advertising for a burglary." He went back in and his wife knew it was time for her to go in too. "The Ben and Jerry's'll melt," she said. "I'll tell him you were here if you want."

"The envelope will be fine." He passed the empty thing through the mail slot.

Rook gave the house a quick, but thorough examination. There was no hint of a burglar alarm. No window contacts, window stickers, or signs. He drove around to the rear and came up to the back of Dunmoore's from the opposite direction. The back door lock was standard, and he could pic-eze it open in a matter of seconds.

Driving through the neighborhood, Rook looked for any

spots that might lead to something. There was a neighborhood bar, "The Ruby," but that wasn't open yet. At a Gas and Go he asked the counterman about the driver who sideswiped him coming out of Dunmoore's development. That got Rook nowhere as did stops at a nearby hardware store and at Reese's barber shop, that was just opening. The owner stuttered badly and had nothing to say.

Rook drove back to the playground where Heather Raimondo was snatched. There were two women with children at the swings. Harry Raimondo was leaning against the cyclone fence with his dog. It started to rain and the mothers scurried. Rook checked the mileage on his odometer. Dunmoore's place was almost equidistant from the playground and the flower monument by the side of the road.

17

"Maybe he'll stop to take a crap, Jimmy. Or feed his other end." Chick said. "There's that rib place on the way to the M.E.'s. Raddichio worked that job when them assistants were stealing from the dead. Seems everybody ate there. We could stop on the way or take Island Avenue and be waiting at Nessel's for sure."

"I don't want to lose him, brother. I gotta collect the evidence and bring it back to the house. I don't want them to have it."

"Nessel or the Feds?" Chick asked.

"This is my case and I don't want any college boys thinking it's theirs. Nessel's as likely to foul it up, Crime Scene not showing and all. He does the autopsy or whatever and he's as likely to lose the P.E. as anybody."

Salerno made a hard turn. "I'm betting your instincts, Chick. There's nothing better to tempt a man with a dead kid in his truck than a plate of ribs and chili fries."

Misher took out a small fingernail file and began pushing back his cuticles. "The doc who was seeing my old man, Nessel reminds me of him in a way. The size, you know. My mother hated him bad. We couldn't convince her otherwise. She blamed him for my old man's death until the day she died. 'Don't get me that Ben Casey', she said over and over. She had them confused, him and the curly headed Jew."

"Jaffe," Salerno told him. "Sam Jaffe."

"Don't remember no Doc Jaffe, Jimmy."

"That was the actor's name, Chick." He swung into the right hand lane.

"Right as rain, brother," Chick called out. Parked against the side of the one story stucco restaurant was the Medical Examiner's van. "They love this place, Jimmy, them M.E. guys. How do you want to handle this?"

"You go in, Chick. He didn't see you. I need about a half-hour." Salerno put on a pair of latex gloves. "Keep him in there."

"No problem. Even if I got to cuff him to the table. You want me to bring you anything?"

"The chili fries sound good, partner. And a ginger ale."

Detective Misher adjusted his tie and went into the place. It was all black and white, the floors, booths and the big blocks on the tile floor. He saw the man his partner described sitting at the counter. The driver, whose name was Corson, was engrossed in a basket of barbecue wings, licking the sauce off his fingers. The handle of the frosted mug in front of him was slick with it.

Misher badged the man next to him and took the stool. "Let's take a booth," he said.

Corson salted his fries. "I don't know you."

"You don't want to, buddy boy. You don't want to know anybody from the Inspector General's office." Chick could see the man tense. "Now let's have a little chat."

"Maybe I should call my union rep before I talk to any-body."

Misher leaned over and took one of the wings. "Tasty," he said. "Maybe tomorrow your name's in the paper and your face is on television. Maybe, maybe. Now, let's have that chat." He took a sip of the driver's beer."Maybe nothing happens."

They moved to the booth that faced away from the parking lot. The waiter came over. "Order of ribs, sauce on the side and a pitcher of Bud. Bring my friend here a clean glass."

He turned to the driver, "You've been the subject of a time-motion study. I figure you're on the clock now, which could mean a theft of time and services or it could mean nothing. You paying full freight for your dinner?" He took out his pad and pen.

"I don't think I should say anything. You got ID?" he dared.

The beer arrived. Chick poured them each a glass. "I show you my shield, I'm here. We chat and have a brew, I'm not."

Corson drank quickly. "I've had enough shit this night to hold me for a lifetime."

"You mean back at the crime scene, Forbidden Drive?"

"You know about that?"

Chick shook his head. "Rotten deal."

"I'm right in the middle. In the middle of shit."

Chick dipped one of the ribs. "Not while we're eating, will ya?"

"Sorry." The driver poured himself another beer.

Salerno was in the van collecting physical evidence. Part of his mind was open so he could do it and access his sense impressions. Part of it was closed so he wouldn't go crazy.

He took a narrow spatula from his inside jacket pocket and a roll of wide transparent tape from his coat. He used them to collect the fibers, hairs and residue from the outside of the body bag which could contaminate his subject. He did this twice before he unzipped the bag, running the tape on the teeth of the zipper to make sure he had gotten everything. After changing his gloves, he brought out Sandy Jelks and laid her on the rubber body bag.

Rigor mortis had set in and her skin was cold. He measured her. She was four feet, one and weighed about fifty pounds. The Polaroid gave him good shots from three feet out. He used the first pack of film to shoot her in the robe from front to back, top to bottom.

Salerno examined her exposed skin for bruises, marks, and gross physical evidence. There were marks around her neck and on her left arm where the killer had grabbed her up. He used the transparent tape to pick up any hair or fibers off her body. There were a number of white cotton fibers on the body, but they would likely be useless because they were so common, and some visible hairs, a few short black ones, which Salerno figured came from the inside of the body bag. He combed her hair. She had lots of curls which made this difficult.

After taking scrapings from under her nails, he examined her more closely. There was a healed abrasion below her left knee and what looked like a faded bruise on her buttocks. He thought about checking for semen, but he had no slides and the M.E. would be taking smears from her vagina and rectum.

Then he saw what he had missed before. A carpet fiber

in the curls at the base of her head. Carpet fibers were almost never enough to convict anybody. Sometimes, they had statistical weight like in the Atlanta serial killings. But in this case, it would make all the difference. "I got you, you son of a bitch," Salerno said out loud. "I got you."

Salerno bagged the girl and paged his partner.

Chick told the van driver that he'd get back to him. When they were in their unmarked. Misher offered the chili fries which his partner ignored. "You get anything?"

Salerno floored the accelerator, throwing cinders up from the parking lot. "I got a carpet thread, partner. The lab gives us what we want, it's going to lead us to a baby killer. The fucking piano man, Chick. The fucking piano man."

"A stake in his heart, Jimmy."

"No doubt about that, my brother. No doubt about that at all.

Detective James Salerno chewed two peppermints and roared out onto the highway.

18

When Inspector Zinn arrived at Forbidden Drive, Lefko met him first, angling to go home. "You want me to wait until Traffic gets here, boss or…"

"It's going to be a long night, Detective."

"Already that, boss, the Feds being here and all. But we got all but an official ID. The vic matched the photo the parents gave me."

"What I want you to do, Gene, is go over to the Jelks'. Right now nobody knows who the vic is except the guy who did her."

"You think maybe her parents did it, Inspector?"

"Nothing surprises me, detective. What I want you to do is see how they're doing. And I don't want them going anywhere. The Feds treat you alright? Any problems?"

"Salerno and them went at it, but they didn't push Jimmy around." He manufactured a sneer. "College boys should mind their own business."

Zinn knew that Detective Lefko lived near the Jelks and that a pit stop could turn into three hours. "Call me from there in thirty minutes, Gene," he told him.

"I'm saddling up, boss."

With Lefko gone, there was just the blue and white up at the barricade and Zinn's car at the entrance to Forbidden Drive. The Inspector called back for Traffic. When they showed up, he would send the cruiser back to patrol duty. "I dispatched a unit, Joe," the sergeant told him. "They're coming from a concert, some heavy metal shit. I'll follow up."

The Inspector looked at his watch. The timer in his head started counting forward and backward. How to get this job going before the Bureau took it from him.

Zinn thought about how Downtown had screwed him. Maybe Downtown wanted the Feds in. If there was federal jurisdiction maybe they escape the bad publicity of reminding everybody how Marie Noe killed eight of her kids in Philly and never served a day. At the least, they should have given him a heads up about the Bureau. His task force and the Feebs were bound to bump heads the way things were going, but no way should he not have been notified in advance. He called Downtown for Deputy Chief Falk.

A supervisor told him that Falk wasn't in. Joe remembered that there was a Fraternal Order of Police meeting, and the FOP was the wrong place to take up the kind of police politics he had in mind. The Inspector looked at his watch again and then called home.

"Don't wait up, Mary."

"You should eat something," she answered. "I made chicken cutlets. I'll make a salad, tomatoes and cucumbers. I'll leave it in the tupperware."

"Make sure you put the alarm on. I'll call you if I'm not coming home."

"Be careful."

You, too, he thought.

Zinn walked over to the mound of leaves that was the last resting place for Sandy Jelks. A screen of shadows was over the sky. He thought he saw something run into the pile of leaves. Maybe a possum.

He surveiled the area slowly so everything he saw could sink in. Then he called back to his precinct through the civilian's access number so he could check on his people. "How are we doing tonight, Sergeant Frann?" the Inspector asked. He could tell it was Frann because of the background sound of fingers tapping on the desk.

"It's Halloween, like every night. We caught one job off of border patrol. Simple MVA turned all funky. The driver's our limp-wristed chiropractor."

"DUI?" the Inspector asked.

"Likely."

"What did he blow?"

"You mean who," the Desk Sergeant quipped, his fingers still going.

Zinn waited silently.

"He wouldn't take no breath analyzer, Inspector. Refused to submit to a blood alcohol neither and would not get out of the car. He wouldn't exit his vehicle because he was overdressed, black stockings, spiked heels, and everything. Except for his wig. It got knocked off when he ran into the light pole. They brought him in ranting and raving."

"Anything else?"

"Yeah, Inspector, there is." Frann paused for dramatic effect. "He looked pretty good."

"Esposito in?"

"I saw her a couple of minutes ago. I think the DUI got better legs."

"Cut the crap, Frann. I'll be back at the house in half an hour," Zinn paused. "ASAC Robert Epps or the Feds pay us a visit before I get back, the farthest they get in is the bullpen. Treat them like any other civilians."

"Any other civilians that are looking to poke you in your ass," the Desk Sergeant answered.

"That's the only right thing you've said." Zinn hung up.

The car from Traffic arrived in fifteen minutes. There were two officers in 103 car. It was a salt and pepper team. Jack Keith, who had been in Traffic for twenty years, was behind the wheel. Riding with him was a woman he hadn't seen before. She had the whitest skin Zinn had ever seen, like a sheet of paper.

"112 got wracked pretty good, Inspector. It looks like it'll be just us," Keith told him. "Me and my partner here. It's her first night out." The rookie nodded and the Inspector nodded back.

"We got to secure the scene, and I think we might have some Federal visitors."

"They been by, Inspector?"

"They've been by."

"I can handle it. I'll put her up there directing traffic and angle my car at the park entrance so I got everything in view. No college boys going to get where they don't belong."

"I don't believe they will," the Inspector said.

Joe Zinn drove back to his precinct. For a couple of blocks the streets were wet. A blue and white was double-parked on Crittenden Street. As he approached, another pulled up behind it. Zinn stopped alongside. "Everything under control?"

The officer nodded and hurried up the steps of the house with the open door.

When the Inspector arrived at the station, he parked under cover in the rear, but walked around and came in through the main door so that everyone would know he was on board. The Desk Sergeant was drumming his fingers and riding one of the young patrolmen about needing some chiropractic treatment. He shut up when he saw the boss.

Zinn went up the front stairs and took the long way so he could get a look at everything. When he got to his office he checked to see that he had a clean shirt, underwear, and socks for the morning. He took an envelope of dehydrated tomato soup from his desk.

On the way to the coffee room for some hot water, he saw Lieutenant Esposito coming down the hall. His Information Officer did have a great figure.

She saw him and came over. "Can I meet with you, boss?"

"My office." They walked back together, but with the Inspector in front.

"Door open or closed, boss?"

"Close it, please, blinds open. Anything to report?"

"The police writer called twice from the Inquirer," Esposito answered. "The second time he asks what we're hiding and what the Feds are doing here."

"What did you tell him?"

"I told him I was uninformed. That confused him."

The Inspector poured the dehydrated soup and boiling water. "He probably won't call again tonight. If he does, ask him how his drunk driving school's going."

"You're kidding me, boss." Then she added, "We got a call from Channel 10."

"No doubt our persistent newspaper reporter's girlfriend."

"That weasel and Lisa Kirkpatrick?"

"You gave her nothing, you won't hear from either one of them until morning. We're going to have a statement to issue by six A.M. so Assistant Special Agent Epps can have it with his morning coffee. You'll need your overtime signed for."

Zinn sipped his soup and began to brief her while he looked for a napkin. "We'll have a visit tomorrow morning from the Feebs. It looks like we found Sandy Jelks. We've got a Task Force set up, but two from the Bureau were already at the scene."

"I got my team together," she answered.

"Go on."

"I got the tech assigned to report early, and my clerk-typist, is going to give me a hand."

"How's that?"

"She'll do her regular duty, but she's helping me out. She's waiting to hear about the test for the Academy."

"I don't want her doing police work, Esposito. And also with your tech, he's got the time in and he knows the job, but remember you're the Lieutenant. What I want is two press releases ready to go. One, we found the Jelks girl and one that addresses our continuing investigation. In both we're talking about the Task Force under my direction. Any questions?"

"This will be my first interaction with the ASAC, Inspector. I hear he's a snake. How do I handle him?"

"He might take an indirect approach with you."

Esposito wasn't sure what that meant, but nodded. "Any forensics in yet, boss?"

"No." Zinn said. He stood up, which meant the meeting was over. When she left his office, he looked at his watch. He could stretch out on the couch or catch a couple of hours at home.

Zinn walked out to "the pit". There were six metal desks, two pairs of two facing each other, one with a computer, and a stand-alone which had become a repository for closed files that should have been sent to storage. He could put Lefko at the stand-alone. The shift overlap would have to use the computer desk now that Salerno would probably be living on the job.

Joe thought about eating a donut. The taste of it came into his mouth, the Communion wafer to turn a world of bloody garbage into something they could live with. The Inspector lay down for a while and tried to sleep. It was going to be a long night and tomorrow things were only going to get worse.

19

Molly Hearn slept with the vaporizer at her bed. The little girl's mother felt her head and sat with her.

"I got to go," her boyfriend called from the bottom of the steps. Julie came out to tell him hush and then went back in her daughter's room to close the blinds. As she did, she saw headlights move by. "That selfish prick," she thought. "He couldn't wait." But when she came back down, Frank was standing in the doorway.

"Molly alright?" He stubbed out his cigarette on the outside wall.

"She's a little warm. If she has a fever in the morning, I'll take her to Dr. Varker. I'll call in sick."

"I thought her father was supposed to get her. Isn't Tuesday his night?"

"Let's not go there, Frank. And would you come inside?"

"You think I'd gone?" His smile showed his crooked teeth.

Julie smoothed her blondish hair away from her face. "I saw a car pull away."

"I'm still here, Julie girl. Must have been from down the block." He followed her back into the house.

"You want me to fix you something?" she asked.

"I got to be in work in an hour. Just enough time to rock your world." He put his arms around her.

Julie pulled away a bit. "I don't feel right, Frank, with Molly upstairs sick and all."

He rubbed against her. "You said she was okay. Maybe I can change your mind."

Julie laughed her little laugh.

Frank pulled her down and she went with him.

Inspector Zinn was napping on the short couch in his office, when an irate call from the Medical Examiner woke him up.

"What are you doing to me, Joe?"

"What are you talking about?"

"What am I talking about! I'm talking about you involving me with the Federal Government, Joe. I'm talking about the FBI calling me at home to roust me."

"I have no idea what you're talking about, Sam. You want to let me in on what you're ranting about." The Inspector changed his socks as he spoke.

"I've got two calls because of you, Joe. One of them's bad and the other's awful. And you're in the middle of both of them."

Zinn could hear the Medical Examiner exhaling smoke angrily. "What the hell are you talking about, Doctor?"

"First, you shanghai one of my transport people. I already heard from his shop steward and the union's lawyer. Then I get another call at home, but this time it's the fucking Federal Bureau of Investigation. Says I'm conspiring with you to obstruct justice and that's a Federal crime and that I had better not touch the DOA, which I gather you must have done because I had one of my people do an exam and there's no physical evidence on the body to speak of."

"Sam, I have no idea whatsoever what you're talking about. I think you're working too hard. Take some time off. Do some of your wood carving. Take a pill or whatever."

Jimmy Salerno was at home on the couch. He got the call on the first ring.

"My office," Zinn told him.

"I'll be there in a half hour, boss."

"Good," the Inspector said.

"Good," Salerno answered. His wife had gone to bed early. He had a cup of instant coffee and left a note on the kitchen sink.

Chick Misher was watching an old Jeff Chandler movie when Salerno called him, "The boss called. I'll be by in fifteen minutes."

"Good, Jimmy. For a minute there, I thought it was the Executioner. She hasn't called me to break my balls in at least a day. We've been divorced eight years and she's still killing me." Misher changed into a navy blazer and a pair of charcoal slacks with a crease that could slice a ham. He was ready right on the dot.

Inspector Zinn called Gene Lefko at the Jelks'. "You were supposed to call in when you got there."

"I thought you were kidding me, boss. I mean that you were talking not literally."

"What does that mean, Detective? It means you're showing me your fancy footwork, Gene."

"No, really, Inspector. I got here early. I stopped home, changed my shirt, and I'm on the job. I'm here at the Jelks'."

"And?"

"It's what you would expect, Inspector. The place is a

train wreck. The mother had to be sedated." Lefko stopped to look at his notes and then went on, "She took Lorzepam. The doctor just prescribed it. The father is running around like a maniac. He's about ready for sedation himself. The neighbor was over for a while, reading nursery rhymes to the boy, but she's gone. They're waiting for Mrs. Jelks' sister."

"C'mon back in. I'll see that the sector car gets over there. You get anything else?"

"Nothing more than I told you."

"Gene…"

"Yes, boss?"

"Don't do your dancing when you work for me."

Lefko knew that the Inspector meant it. He made another try at Donald Jelks, but came up with the same story as before. As the sector car arrived, Lefko told the Jelks' that it was still too early to think the worst.

Joe Zinn washed, shaved, and changed the rest of his clothes. There was a knock at his door. It was his Task Force: Salerno, Misher, Gene Lefko, and Vanessa Esposito. Salerno had his tie on.

"First, nothing in this room leaves this room," the Inspector said "By now everybody here knows we got a baby killer. The new DOA hasn't been officially ID'd yet, although it's the Jelks' girl. As you know, Assistant Special Agent Epps has got this on his plate. I figure I'll have the paperwork in the A.M., and, if I know Epps, he'll be here before eight o'clock just so he can stick it to us."

The three detectives had something bad to say about

Epps, and the Inspector let them go at it. Then he brought them around, "Epps got the M.E. spooked. No way we're going to get anything from Nessel now. If we're lucky, Sam will mail us a copy of his report. More likely, the Feds will do their own pathology, which we'll never see." He sat down. "I don't want you getting jammed up behind all this politics, people," Zinn said. "If anybody's going to be in the middle of this bag of crap, it should be me. Any problems?"

"I got work to do, boss. I'm not good at politics," Salerno said.

Lefko looked over to see if Jimmy was done. "Me either. I don't know exactly how you do things here. I didn't know whether you wanted me to submit my reports to the Task Force or you, Inspector."

"I haven't decided where to go with the paperwork, Gene. What do you have?"

"Okay, I was at the Jeltz's. The mother is hysterical. They have her on them pills to quiet her down."

"Who?" Salerno asked. "Who is 'they', Gene?"

"The husband told me that the family doctor called it in." Lefko looked at his notepad. "Doc's name was 'Mooar'." He spelled it. The husband's trying to hold it together. It looks to me he was in Rochester for work when the girl gets grabbed up. I didn't have time to check with his hotel and the airlines, but it don't look like it could have been him."

He looked back at his notes. "I get there, a neighbor's with them, Rose Colanzi, from next door. She brought them some kind of casserole. I interviewed her. Been next door for years. No kids. She works for a foot doctor. Then the sector car comes like you said."

Inspector Zinn adjourned the meeting.

Salerno took his partner aside. "Heather Raimondo's mother worked for a podiatrist, Chick."

"I'll check it out, if you want, brother."

Nodding at his partner, he went back in.

"You got physical evidence, Jimmy?"

"We're going to get us a baby killer, boss. I got carpet thread I found in the vic's hair. It's got to have come from the piano player's place. I'd know that ugly color anywhere."

The Inspector looked at his watch. Jimmy knew what that meant. They had until Epps showed up to handle the job themselves. Then it was the Feds'.

When Detective Salerno came out of the Inspector's office, Gene Lefko was still there. "You want to grab a brew gents?" he asked.

"Jimmy's going to run me home, Gene. My tranny's shot."

"Right," Lefko said. "I'm going to clock out." He looked at his watch. "I was going to swing around the Jeltzs' once more, but tomorrow's going to be a busy day."

"The Dancing Machine," Salerno said as he left the Squad with his partner. They went down to the unmarked. Salerno had the keys, and didn't give them up even though it wasn't his turn to drive. Chick knew Jimmy was pumped, so he let it pass.

They drove out of the precinct lot and swung around the block. When they came back, Lefko's Pontiac was still in the lot. "Fucking guy is probably asleep on his new desk," Salerno said.

"Or playing suck-up with the boss, partner."

"We'll give him ten more minutes, Chick. That's it."

They pulled into the small alley across the street from the station house. Lefko was out in a minute. Salerno pulled their unmarked back into the lot and they went back to the squad.

Misher grabbed body armor for the two of them and checked the batteries on the squad's video camera. Salerno took some legal-looking papers from the bottom drawer of his desk. They would serve the immediate purpose of a search warrant even though they were actually for a Sheriff's sale held six years ago. He also brought his tape recorder and an old piece of portable dictation equipment that they could pass-off as a lie detector.

Last, they checked their weapons and put fresh loads in their service pieces. Out in the car they checked their back-ups and the old Ruger .22 that could serve as a throw-down.

"The carpet thread," Salerno said as he started the engine. "I got it bagged up. It's the same fucking kind on those step things the kids used for their piano lessons. The same dirty piss color and the same kind of pile. I don't need a lab to tell me that." He took a roll of Tums from his pocket and bit off three or four.

Salerno pushed it hard and slid through a couple of red lights.

"Easy, partner," Chick said. Then he tried to defuse the tension. "*Jeltz* he says. The Dancing Machine says he's going back to the *Jeltz's*. Gene's been out there what, two days and he don't know it's *Jelks*."

"That's Gene." Salerno made a hard right.

"Switch hitter."

"Gene?"

"No, Jeltz. Used to play shortstop for the Phillies."

"Right. Jeri-curled 'bro' couldn't hit his weight. Couldn't carry Larry Bowa's jock strap. No fire in his belly."

Chick adjusted his ankle holster. "Bowa should've been the manager two years ago."

"Political shit."

"Right, like what's jamming up the boss."

It started to rain. They were half way there.

Salerno went on, "Fuck Epps. That empty suit probably never made a street collar in his life. We should've locked up this piece of shit, Dunmoore, before."

"Behind what, Jimmy? We didn't have any P.E. then. Now you got that physical evidence, we'll put a stake in his heart."

Salerno turned the wipers on high. "The prick's probably sleeping like a baby. Still got blood on his hands. All over them weird fingers of his."

"Nothing's going to save him now," Chick said. "We got his evil ass. Put a stake in his heart."

The rain slowed down, and as they came across Route 3 a warm wind, strange for that time of year, blew in from the east. Salerno drove by the front of the garden apartments and then made a pass at the back. There were two lights on inside Dunmoore's townhouse, one downstairs and the other in the back of the second floor.

Jimmy pic-ezed the front door as his partner whispered, "Open up, police."

They were inside in moments with their guns drawn. The place was empty.

20

The incongruity of the pristine house with its pall of terror was not lost on Robert Epps, but his demeanor was as smooth as a maitre d'. "The total resources of the Federal Bureau of Investigation are committed to you, Mr. and Mrs. Jelks."

Donald took the ASAC's card.

Mrs. Jelks stared.

"I understand that this is a most difficult time for you," Epps went on. "I want to tell you that I shall be involved in this matter personally. We're putting what we call a 'full field' on this. Starting tomorrow morning, members of the Bureau's special units will be here to meet with you and assist me." He pushed his red hair back off of his forehead.

"We've already spoken to the police," Mr. Jelks said. He was a doughy man and he fidgeted when he spoke.

"I'm sure that will be quite helpful." Renaldo Dellum walked up close to Jelks. "I am the primary agent on this case. Part of my case responsibility is to see that someone is immediately available to you, 24/7."

Mrs. Jelks went to the stairs and stood there. Donald walked towards the door. "We'll be alright. She'll sleep through the night with the pills they're giving her."

"I'll have someone outside," Epps told him, "Primary Agent Dellum here or someone directly under his control. In the morning, Agent Eileen Handler will be here from our 'FO', our field office. She's a fine agent, and she'll be a help to your wife."

He went over to Mrs. Jelks. "The United States Government will do its best for your daughter." Epps put his hand on her shoulder, but, she did not react.

"Can you make a list of your daughter's friends? That would be a big help," Dellum said.

"The thing that would be a help is Sandy coming home. That happens, doesn't it?" Mr. Jelks reached for where his cigarettes usually were. "It happens, doesn't it? The police we spoke to said it happens all the time."

"Who would that be?" Dellum offered one of his smokes.

Donald pulled the cloud of tar and nicotine into his lungs. "Who?" he repeated.

"Who were the policemen you spoke to?" the agent repeated.

The cigarette relaxed Jelks a bit. "First, the policeman who came when we first called. He was in uniform. I don't remember his name. Then a Detective Lefko. And his boss."

"And who would that be—Lefko's boss?"

"I assume he was his boss. Inspector Zinn, Joseph Zinn. Detective Lefko came by again tonight." Jelks crushed out his half-smoked cigarette.

"Anyone else come by, Mr. Jelks?" Dellum asked. "Or call? Did anyone call about your daughter?"

Jelks sat down in their flowered armchair, then stood up again. His wife stood mute, looking blankly out the window. "Nobody called. Detective Lefko said that's often a sign that Sandy is hiding or something. That happens a lot," he said.

He reached to his pocket again. "Which is why it's so bad that you're here. I guess that means…"

"It doesn't necessarily mean anything, Mr. Jelks," Epps said.

Dellum offered another cigarette. Jelks shook his head.

The ASAC concluded the meeting, "I'll see that an agent waits outside. I'll talk to you tomorrow morning. In the meantime, get some sleep. If you need anything or remember anything, someone is here for you night and day."

Epps and Dellum left, the agent walking a bit ahead so he could catch a smoke before they got into the car. "I'll tell them tomorrow that the DOA in the park is their kid," he said as they drove away.

Epps finger-combed his hair. "That'll be fine, Renaldo."

Julie Hearn sat inside her cubicle at Darby Precision. The space was like her own private room even though there were a dozen more cubicles all around her. She had put up pictures of Molly and herself and one with Frank that they had taken at Disney.

It was a good day so far. She was learning the new computer program, so that soon she would be able to not only do correspondence, but would be able to trace and confirm orders. That meant she'd have a real shot at promotion.

Julie had two plants on her desk. The one from Molly had a popsicle stick with hearts on it. She felt the potting soil to see if it needed water. The phone rang. It was the school. Molly had seemed well enough in the morning, but now her temperature was 102°.

The way they did things at work, Julie had to take a whole day's sick leave because she was leaving before noon. Even though her ex was a jerk, it was times like this that she wished he lived closer than three hours away. And she wasn't ready to ask Frank to take time off yet. Julie didn't want to chase him away.

She made the trip in less than fifteen minutes. Her daughter's face was flushed. "You sick again, pumpkin? I'll get you some ginger ale. And we can go home, and I'll make you all snuggly."

Molly put her head down when she got into the car. "Am I going to have to get a stick put down my throat?"

"Does it hurt, pumpkin?"

"I'm tired, Mommy."

There was a convenience store up ahead. "I'll make you some soup with X's and O's when we get home. I'm going to go in here and then be right out. I'll bring you a candy treat."

Julie Hearn went in to get the ginger ale, two cans of soup and some hard candy for Molly to suck on. After she paid and was half-way out, she realized she was going to run out of cigarettes and went back in. Other than the twenty she kept folded up behind her driver's license, she was out of cash. But Frank would be by and the support check was due. Julie Hearn knew that she'd make it. She always did.

When they got home, Julie called the pediatrician. It was Wednesday, which meant Dr. Varker wasn't in. The doctor on call told her it was probably a virus and to give Tylenol or Advil and a cool bath if her temperature spiked. Julie gave Molly the Tylenol and some ginger ale and put her down to sleep. If Molly felt better when she woke up, she would make her a grilled cheese and they could have that for their dinner. It was just after three o'clock.

Julie looked in on her daughter in twenty minutes. She pulled her blanket up, kissed her, and went back downstairs, hoping that the mail and her support check had arrived. She did not notice the car that was parked across the street.

Molly Hearn felt safe in her canopied bed with the ruffled pink skirt around the edges and the shelf of stuffed animals where she could see them.

It was still dark out when she awoke. Her fever had broken. Molly called out three times. She knew that the monitor next to her bed meant that she would be heard. "Mommy, come here. I want you."

After the third time, her mom did come across the hall. She was wearing a blue flannel shirt that went past her waist. Julie shook back her new hairstyle, she had gotten it done like Kathy Lee, and put her forehead against her daughter's. "Your fever's all gone. Let's use the bathroom. Then you can go back to sleep. I think you can go to school tomorrow."

"Is Uncle Frank here, Mommy?"

"Why, pumpkin?"

"Because your door is closed. I went and looked."

"I guess it was. Well, it shouldn't be."

Molly sat on the toilet. "It's okay, Mommy. You could still hear me on the microphone."

Julie gave her some more Tylenol. "Here, chew these up. They're the grape kind."

"Can I sleep in your bed?" Molly asked.

"I'll stay with you."

"The whole night?"

"Until you're sleeping tight." She took her daughter by the hand to her room.

"So the bugs don't bite?"

146

"So the bugs don't bite." Julie pulled the covers up to Molly's chin. "The bad old germs don't like it when it's warm and toasty."

She sat with Molly until her child dozed. Then she kissed her on the cheek. "I'll check on you three times."

The little girl opened her eyes. "And this one doesn't count?" which is what she asked every night.

"And this one doesn't count," her mother said.

Molly fell asleep, and from time to time she went in and out of dreams. At last it seemed that she was floating and then that she was going for a ride. She awoke in a strange place in a warm bath.

"Here's something clean to wear," she heard as practiced hands grabbed her neck.

21

Misher was the more talkative of the two detectives, but he only offered "fuck me" as they drove away from Stewart Dunmoore's empty apartment. He said it twice as Salerno fumed.

They had been on the road for almost twenty minutes before Salerno said anything, "No way, Chick. No way. No Dunmoore. No clothes, belongings. Nothing. But there's no way I let him get away."

"We got 'Uncle' in here brother," Misher said. "By tomorrow they'll be looking at anything we do as obstruction. And the boss, no way he crosses the Bureau over this."

Jimmy wore his watch with the face on the inside of his wrist and he turned his thick arm so he could see the time. "I'm running this straight through until somebody grabs me hard and pulls me off."

"I got some statements on my flyer case tomorrow," Chick said. "Nobody's been working on the roof that long takes a fall like that. Word on the street is he had it coming. And I got a Preliminary Hearing, but I got a snitch who works 24/7 and owes me bad. Maybe we should grab something to eat and I'll call him and let him know I'm in the market for info on Stewart."

Salerno nodded and turned at the next corner.

Jimmy and Chick sat in their usual booth in Bill Higgins' bar, looking out at the late shoppers wheeling their carts from the supermarket. Higgins had been on the job long enough to know when things weren't going right.

"I got something to cheer you two fine members of the Blue Line," Big Bill said. He angled himself into the booth to accommodate his belly. "Sally," he called. "Bring us over your special." He turned back to Salerno and Chick. "Wait 'til you see this," he added.

Sally Keesal came over from the bar with a bottle and three glasses. She arrived at their table with a new walk and perfect pair of brand new 38 D's.

The two detectives were staring, and Sally and her boss were loving it. "You like them, gentlemen? Compliments of the management. They're a gift from Mr. Higgins." She undulated when she walked away. "If I'm a good girl, I get a new bottom for Christmas."

"Jesus H. Christ!" Misher said. "They're beautiful."

"You should see them up close," Higgins told them.

"In a pig's eye, Bill," Salerno said. "In a pig's eye."

"Damn if I don't, Jimmy. I got to check on my investment." Big Bill poured them each a cold one.

"Investment? You ain't never going to get any of that."

"Well, maybe I am, Chick. And maybe I'm not. But the arrangement I got is once a month I get to check them out. See that they're all even and what-not."

"Once a month you're telling me. It's like you're married, once a month."

"What did it cost you, Billy? Ten, twelve grand?" Salerno asked.

Higgins poured himself a drink. "After tax dollars, it's going to run me forty-five hundred."

"What do you mean 'after tax dollars'? No way you can write this off."

"I get the sign out front fixed, Jimmy. I write that off. I get a new juke box, that's a deduction. I write this off the same way."

Misher shook his head. "So your shyster accountant writes it off. Still, the only one's going to get any of that is her weasel boyfriend."

"Say that's true, Chick. Suppose it is. It's still a good thing to have around, ain't it?" Bill Higgins maneuvered himself back out of the booth. "Don't you feel hardy with Sally and them new melons around. It's like you're getting Viagra on the house."

"I wouldn't know about that," Misher told him.

Jimmy Salerno picked up the menu. "How's the meat loaf, Bill?"

"We sold out. The chicken platter's real good."

"The beans canned?"

"You know I don't use no canned vegetables. They're fresh frozen."

The detectives ordered their platters and Chick went to call his informant.

"Viagra?" he asked when he got back. Your face kinda got red when he brought it up, Jimmy. You on that?"

"Christ, Chick, I just took it once. My blood pressure and all."

Misher tucked a napkin in his shirt. "So?"

"So. It was weird, partner."

Sally came over with their salads, wedges of lettuce with smaller wedges of tomato and carrot shavings.

"Thank you. Thank you," Chick said. "I love melons with my meal." "Weird, how weird?" he asked his partner when the waitress left.

Salerno's face got red. "Well, the wife's asleep. You know, and I'm half asleep. But the other 'Jimmy', he's standing at attention like a rookie at his first roll call."

"Otherwise?"

"Otherwise…it's fine, partner. Let's drop it."

Misher nodded, sorry that he had pursued the subject.

By the time they were done their chicken and the coffee came, the warmth of the meal and the entertainment from the new tits had worn off. Young Billy and his wife had come in. She came over to give them their check, and she was as mean as usual.

Salerno shoved his coffee cup aside, "Back to the bag-of-crap reality, partner. It's a bad situation. We got a baby killer in our town, my brother. And the Feds are going to fuck that up. Plus Downtown taking us off the case the way they did. Not to mention this New York private the boss tells me about."

Chick took the napkin out of his shirt and wiped the table crumbs away from him. "You get hurt worse by somebody inside with a pen than you do by somebody outside with a gun."

Salerno reached for the check, but his partner took it and held his cup up for a refill. Young Billy's wife ignored him. "She's bad, Jimmy. She's as bad as Sally's new tits are good. Now you know why I'm batching it all these years." He got up to go over to the counter. "You want a piece of pie or something, partner? Melon pie maybe."

Jimmy grimaced. "We're out of here, Chick."

Then he saw Rook come into the bar. Young Billy came over to say that a New York cop wanted to buy him a drink and Rook walked over.

Salerno's face was a dark red. "You piss in my yard, Mr. PI, the best you are is going to be busted. If you had a half a brain you'd go back up to Jew York and do whatever you were doing before you became a rent-a-cop."

"Put your petty shit on hold," answered Rook. "We exchange any intel. Whoever gets close, you grab up the guy."

"And you grab your fee."

"I call my client…"

"Sceevone," Salerno replied.

"The baby killer murdered his little girl," Rook said.

"So we got a rent-a-cop with a sense of justice? I don't think so."

"I'm going to work it through Jack O'Meara. Give you guys a little insulation."

Misher came over. "Everything okay here, partner?"

"We're out of here, Chick. This is the worst shit sandwich I've seen in in twenty years. " They headed for the door without turning back.

"Hey, Salerno," Rook called. "I thought you wanted to close this case."

"You are a pain in the ass," Salerno told him.

"You got that right," Rook said.

22

Rook tried Jack O'Meara at home, but Carolyn answered the phone. A tea kettle whistled in the background.

"Just cleaning out the frig. That's what I do mostly—clean."

"I tried for your husband over at the Bridge, but they said he wasn't scheduled. You got a number for him, Carolyn? I couldn't find him at the usual watering holes."

"They suspended him, Lucas. Drinking on the job. Maybe you could do something. He has a room over in Castor Gardens. I'll get you his number."

She read it to him from the paper she kept in her drawer with the coupons. No need to put it up on the frig with the other numbers, reminding her that her husband lived somewhere else.

Rook would set up the meeting: Jack himself, Salerno.

He called Salerno, who was not happy to get the phone call.

"Sorry we didn't get to chat last time, James. I think we should meet," Rook said. "Like I said, me, you and Jack."

"I think you should go fuck yourself, like I said."

"You are a douche bag, Salerno. In the meantime, let's do this."

"Do what?" Jimmy rooted through his desk drawer looking for a lifesaver.

"Me, Jack O'Meara, you and your partner, back at your watering hole."

"First, we aren't doing nothing. Second, stay out of Bill Higgins' place. You don't belong there."

"Maybe we help you with your case."

"You guys close?" Jimmy asked him "That may not be so healthy for Jack, working close with you."

Rook took a deep breath. "Think about the baby killer."

There was no response. "I'll be back at Higgins' tonight, Salerno. Maybe with my help you won't have any more little girls turning up dead."

Rook knew that at this point, he didn't have that many cards in play. Ralphie Cheese was just a scumbag that O'Meara knew needed another beating. His spadework had turned nothing new. That left Dunmoore, Harry, Jimmy Salerno. First, he'd make a last run at Heather's father. Salerno no doubt had looked at the parents hard, and there was nothing to indicate either one of them had killed Heather, but Rook wasn't ready to let Harry go.

The playground where the girl was grabbed up was on the way. Rook drove by. It was starting to get dark earlier and earlier. There were some kids shooting baskets and a couple with their baby. Sirens went off in the distance and dogs began to howl.

He drove around the playground twice and then parked at the end of an adjacent street. Sometimes the shark came back to the same spot to feed. Rook sat and waited. One of the finer skills of police work. After an hour and a half he drove off to the Raimondo's.

Harry was getting out of his car as Rook came around the corner. He popped the trunk and walked around to get the bags of groceries. The dog wasn't with him.

Rook flexed his bad leg. The time in the car had stiffened it up and he didn't want his client to see him limp.

Raimondo was at the gate. He turned towards Rook with his hands full. "How ya doin'?"

Rook reached around and opened the gate. Harry nodded. "Come on in. Maybe you got something to tell me."

They went down the path past the peonies. The dog was not in the fenced yard or barking from inside. As they came up to the back door, Mrs. Raimondo opened it. She was in her housecoat and slippers. "I'm not dressed," she said, hurrying down the hall.

"Sit down, Mr. Rook. I got to put some of this away." The first bag had three heads of Romaine and a package of chicken that was leaking. "Jesus Christ, you can't get nothing done right no more. I turn my head one minute and they've ruined it. Now all this got to be washed."

The big man dropped the bag into the sink and washed his hands. "I'll put the coffee on." He got a bottle of J&B and two glasses and sat down, his feet reaching for where his dog usually lay. "The dog's at the vet. They got to knock him out to clean his teeth as big as he is." He poured two good drinks. "Tell me something," he said.

"I met with Salerno and his partner."

"A lot of good that'll do. They've been on this before."

"Salerno's still got a passion for this case."

"And that's all he got. My lawyer called me. Castriota, you met him here, I think. He called not ten minutes ago, tells me to tell you to call him when I see you. He has something for you."

Mrs. Raimondo came back with two coffee cups, but Rook had already gotten up. "You take care, Harry, Mrs. Raimondo. I know the way out."

As Rook was leaving, the phone rang. Raimondo picked it up. "It's for you," he said.

Salerno was on the other end. "Jack won't be joining us," he said.

"You talk him out of it?"

"Not really. It's the way things are, New York. You know. It's not healthy being around you."

"Meaning what, Salerno?"

"Meaning two hours ago, Jack O'Meara took a header off the Ben Franklin Bridge."

For a moment Rook felt his mind's forbidden door open. It seemed luminescent. The phone in his hand was pulsing. He saw his brother fall and heard the wailing sound of sirens. Then he pulled himself back.

"You okay, Rook?" Salerno jibed. "You see a ghost or something? Maybe you should get yourself back up the turnpike."

Rook let the comment pass.

"I'll get back up the turnpike, but not until this case is cleared. I'm going to work this job, Jack or no Jack. You want what I get, I'll give it to you. You want a piece of me, I'll be at the O'Meara's to pay my respects."

"The place will be crowded, full up with our people. You don't belong there."

"I'll be by. I don't want you causing any scene for her,

but after the wake, you want me, I'll be easy to find."

"Sure, New York, sure you will. You'll be hiding behind somebody, alive or dead."

Rook clenched his fists. "Brother cop or not, you're over the line, Salerno. You're over the line and you're not going to like what you find."

"Tell me about it, New York," Salerno said, but he had already hung up.

Rook walked around his room and then went out and drove with the windows down. The air was cold rushing by. He listened to it and drove out from the city, passed the swamp land at Essington, a favorite resting place for the suddenly dead.

23

Rook went over to the O'Meara's. He thought somehow the job would be easier in a way without having to work through Jack. Less protocol, policies and procedures. No way was he going to Miranda anybody. No search warrants.

When he got to the house, all the lights were on. There were cars in the driveway and out front, including a cruiser with "DC" on it, meaning the District Commander was there.

The front door was open. A short man smoking a cigar met him at the door. He was older than Rook, maybe his mid-fifties. "No reporters," he said.

"I'm a friend of the family," Rook answered, "Carolyn and Jack."

She was dressed in black, sitting in a black chair. A younger woman, who looked like her sister, sat next to her. A priest came in from the kitchen carrying a dish of macaroni salad and two beers.

Rook leaned over to Carolyn. She smelled old. "I'm sorry for your loss," he said.

She turned towards him. Her skin seemed transparent. "I put this dress on the day our boy got killed. I prayed that I'd never be wearing it again."

The man at the door balanced a paper plate of ham and tomato salad on his lap. Rook nodded to him as he left.

He called Catherine Wren from the car. Her phone rang and rang. She finally picked up and was not happy to hear from him.

"Were you sleeping?"

"No."

"I'm coming over."

"I don't think so," Catherine said.

Rook opened his car window. "I'll be there in twenty minutes."

"I'd rather you don't." She hung up.

Rook drove on. When he arrived, the house was dark. The air was strong with the scent of her lilac bushes.

She opened the door when he rang the bell, but did not let him in. "If you've come to apologize, Lucas…"

"Christ, Catherine, what are you so pissed about?" he asked. "If I've done something wrong…" He walked towards her.

"I'm not going through that anymore."

Rook looked at her.

"Your acting out. I'm not going out for a glass of white wine and coming home with somebody's blood on my clothes."

Rook leaned against the door frame. "What was I supposed to do?"

Catherine still stood in the doorway. "You weren't supposed to get into a fight in the middle of a restaurant. You could have told the manager, called the police."

"They got what was coming to them."

"That's right, they did, Lucas Rook. And they got it from you."

"That's my job. That's what I do. They got the justice they deserved."

"Is that what you think it is—justice? If it is, it's your justice they're getting. Your own 'Lucas Rook' justice."

"And what's wrong with that?" He went over to her, but she turned away.

Catherine shook her head. Her eyes were filled with tears. "What's wrong? What's wrong? It isn't the law's justice. Or morality's. It's your own. Your private justice. That's why I don't want you here. I saw your face when you hurt them."

"My face? They were animals. One of them had a knife. They'd have cut your throat without a second thought."

"You liked it. I never saw it before. I heard it in the sound of your voice. It's always been there, like when you describe the cases you're working on. You're feeding on it, on all the iniquity you can find. It's your sustenance, all that evil."

Rook shook his head. "I was a gold shield detective. I got medals when I got the bad guys off the street. And that's a good thing because they're predators without mercy."

She started to close the door.

"I'm right, and you're wrong." Rook said. "Think about it, Catherine, and when I'm done maybe Heather Raimondo's parents will be able to get some sleep."

"I have thought about it, Lucas Rook and I'm not going to be a part of it anymore."

"A part of what? What?"

Catherine Wren turned away and then back again. "Your anger and your guilt."

"My guilt? My guilt for what?"

"For being the one that's still alive," she told him.

24

Dickie Dimes had no qualms about selling the whereabouts of Stewart Charles Dunmoore more than once. Sometimes he sold the same information three or four times. He smiled when Rook showed him a fifty. It was going to be a profitable business day.

The stoolie stirred his cup of coffee and looked up as the waitress brought him his ham and eggs. "I asked for potatoes, dear."

"You're generous with my money. Now you got something for me or what?" Rook put the bill back in his shirt pocket.

"Sure, sure. But I got to get something in my stomach. I got to eat. I got hypoglycemia. My blood sugar's low, I can't think so good."

"You got two minutes."

Dickie Dimes took four packs of sugar and poured them into his coffee.

"Sure, sure. My guy just told me to expect your call, and I was there to take it, so here we are. You got a badge, identification, something?"

Rook started into his jacket pocket, then reached over and poured the cup of hot coffee into Dickie Dimes' lap. The informant jumped, losing his glasses.

"Jesus Christ! What's wrong with you? This ain't right!" He started to dry himself off with a wad of napkins.

The waitress arrived with the potatoes. Rook took it from her and moved over to sit down next to the snitch. "You open your mouth again, I'm going to take you outside and tune you. Then I'm going to run you in. Put you so deep into the system that by the time you get out, you'll wish you were back in." Rook took a forkful of the scrambled eggs. "Now tell me what you got."

The snitch had his glasses back on. He read this guy as a cop in response to his call to Chick Misher. This meant the other calls he had placed might be answered too, Maybe even a triple sale. This buoyed him. "Sure, sure, Detective. Whatever you say. I was a little confused there for a while. Whatever you need."

"First, I need an address. You got the whereabouts for Stewart Dunmoore?"

"A 'yard' right? Two of them fifties."

Rook took a fork in his hand and feinted with it. Dickie flinched.

"Jesus Christ! Sure, sure. Ann Street, 3212, in Delaware County, Drexel Hill, I think, I've never been there."

"What do you know about that little girl that got grabbed up and strangled about ten months ago, Heather Raimondo? They found her by the side of the road."

Dickie shook his head. "I got nothing on that."

"You like them young, Dickie Boy? Is that the real game you're running?"

The informant held up his hands. "Jesus, no. Christ, I don't do that kind of thing. You think I'm some degenerate, or what? I've got a fiancé and all and a daughter."

"That's too much for me to even contemplate. You got anything else for me?"

The snitch shook his head.

Rook left the fifty dollar bill and the check. "Don't forget to leave the lady a nice tip, Dickie Boy."

While Rook was on his way to Stewart Dunmoore, Chick Misher was meeting with his confidential informant. Dickie Dimes was confused at first. He thought the prick who had just scalded him with coffee and taken a bite of his breakfast was Misher's guy. Now, who he really was didn't matter. All that did matter was that he close the deal at hand. He needed more than another "Grant" because now he needed to get his pants cleaned.

"I called you back, Chick, twice."

"Sorry. I was meeting with the President. Don't yank my chain. What do you got?"

"I got to get something into me, Chick. You know, my blood sugar and all." He picked up the menu.

The Detective took it away from him. "This isn't no date. Gimme what you got or I'm leaving."

"I'm getting faint, Chick. Honest. My memory gets weak. Hypoglycemia, you know. Cup of coffee?"

The detective called the waitress over. He looked at the name embroidered on her uniform. "Two cups of coffee, Florence."

"Can I have a couple of eggs?" Dickie asked. "Bacon."

The waitress wrote that down and started to walk away. "And an order of rye toast," he called.

Misher started to leave. "I told you not to pull my chain, pus boy."

"I got what you want, Chick. Honest. And more."

"And what's that, Dickie boy?"

"I got Stewart Dunmoore's address. I need more than fifty for that since somebody else is wanting that."

"And who else is looking for him, a big black guy in an expensive suit, got a bimbo for a partner?"

"That's another transaction, Chick, who else is looking. And there's the issue of confidentiality." He saw the scowl on Misher's face.

Dickie resigned himself to the original deal. He wrote the Ann Street address.

"And who else is in the market for this info, Dickie?"

"I'll give you that on the house." The informant described Rook but held back that he had also called the Feds. "He's not a nice man. First, I thought he was from your squad, even with the New York accent and all. But then I could tell he wasn't, the way he was disrespecting me and all. You know, not respecting me as a resource."

"Right. You're a national treasure." Chick put the money on the table and left.

Misher called Jimmy and told him he was on the way. He knew it was a four man job to bring in Dunmoore, but the Feds were around and time was running real short. "We got him, Jimmy," he said when he got back to the precinct. "We got the piano man. Let's take him down. I'll pick you up in back. Dress for dinner."

Salerno grabbed two vests, raid jackets, and a shotgun. He took the phony no knock warrant from his desk.

Esposito walked by. "Where you off to?"

"Somebody's funeral," he told her.

"That's a good thing," she answered.

Drexel Hill would take them about twenty-five minutes.

They had to check in with Big Ed Goodstein, the local police chief. Jimmy made the call just as they pulled up to Ann Street, then disconnected himself.

They rolled up on the thirty two hundred block. It was divided by a driveway on one end and the corner at the other. The houses were stucco twins. Some of them had aluminum siding. Dunmoore's didn't. They all had little porches with black iron railings.

Chick drove around back. There was a narrow alley, just wide enough for one car. He parked their unmarked to block one end of the back. "You want the privilege, partner?"

Salerno thumped on the heart plate of his body armor. "Vested up," he answered. "Count to twenty, Chick."

Misher rapped on his vest in response. "Let's get the bad guy. Put a stake in his heart."

"Knock, knock. Police," Jimmy said quietly as he headed around to the front. The house was only four doors down from the driveway, but there was an old woman with a crying child sitting on the third porch. Salerno went quickly down the block behind the parked cars, counting as he walked.

He arrived with eight seconds left and waited in a crouch behind the grey Taurus parked in front. "Seventeen, eighteen, nineteen," up the short path to the three cement steps. He could hear the piano from inside.

Salerno went crashing through the front door as Misher came in the back. "God damn it!" Salerno said. It was too disjointed, too bizarre. Lucas Rook was on the phone. The sounds of "Claire de Lune" came from the stereo. And there swung Stewart Charles Dunmoore, hanging from a yellow nylon rope, his feet dragging on the piano as he swung back and forth, no longer feeling guilt for the death of the unborn child in his mother's womb or the scorn of others for his

165

25

The two detectives had their weapons on Lucas Rook. "Let the phone drop, asshole," Misher said.

Rook didn't move. "I'm calling it in."

"You ain't one of ours, so shut the fuck up!" Salerno told him. "You got this guy," he added, nodding to Chick. "I got the one who's already dead."

Salerno went over to the swinging body. Stewart Charles Dunmoore was in his pajamas. His face was dark and swollen.

A stack of rug-covered bolsters had been piled on the piano. In the middle of that tumbled, make-shift platform was a bolster covered in the yellow carpet that matched the fiber from Sandy Jelks' hair. "Bingo!" Salerno said out loud.

Rook stood with the phone still in his hand. "Your boss said…" he started.

Misher took a step forward. "We told you to shut the fuck up. Put the phone down. Last time I tell you!"

Salerno came back into the kitchen. Asking a cop to give up his gun could easily turn into a life or death situation. "Let's do this nicely," he said slowly and calmly. "Open up your windbreaker and with your left hand, remove your weapon." When Jimmy saw it was a Glock, he added "nice and easy, we don't want no accidental discharge."

Rook removed his gun with two fingers and placed it on the kitchen counter.

"Your back-up," Salerno said. "Put that on the sink."

"And your throw-down," Misher added.

Rook removed his back-up piece. "I don't use a throw-down."

"We'll see, my friend. I'd like you to assume the position, hands on the frig." Salerno patted Rook down while his partner covered them. Jimmy collected both weapons and put them in the dishwasher. "Take a seat over there at the kitchen table and tell us what you're doing at my crime scene. You a friend of my friend in the other room?"

"I got Zinn's clearance, Salerno. He told you."

Salerno's face got red with anger. "You don't belong here. You're going to fuck this up. Just you're being here contaminates the scene."

"Maybe you're a bad guy," Chick added. "We don't like bad guys."

"When you two are done playing bad cop/worse cop, maybe you should call your boss. I got…"

"Maybe you should shut your hole."

"Maybe you got what?" Salerno asked. "Maybe you got murder on your hands."

"I got clearance from your boss to work the Heather Raimondo job."

"In a pig's eye you do. All you got is you lost your brother on the job in New York. Now you're working for them creeps and fouling up at my crime scene."

"Call your boss. The phone works."

"I'm not calling nobody, Rook. So right now you're fucking up my crime scene, and if you didn't off our friend in the other room, you're a material witness."

"I'm putting my hands down. You want to throw shots, you go ahead. On the other hand, I got something you want. So whenever you're done being assholes, let me know and you can clear your case."

"You got nothing," Salerno said. "You had a dead man hanging by his neck. Now I got that. You got nothing."

"I got your case cleared, Salerno. You want it, it's yours, just as I told Zinn. Only thing, I got to call Raimondo like I was about to."

"You ain't calling nobody," Chick said.

"Well, maybe you're right, gents. Maybe I give what I got only to your Chief of D's." Rook sat down.

Salerno reached for his blackjack. "You'll talk to my Chief of Detectives when hell freezes over. You got something, you give it up now."

"I don't want to wind up as a vic, let alone being your material witness. I give over what I got, maybe you…"

The three of them turned at the sound of cars pulling up to the front and back of the townhouse. There were a half dozen heavily armed men on them in moments. They wore blue jackets with big yellow letters. In front was a tall black man. Coming up from behind him was Assistant Special Agent-in-Charge Robert Epps.

"Let's everybody calm down, people," Epps said. "Detectives, let's holster your weapons and let's meet your friends here."

"Your college boys first," Salerno answered.

The ASAC ran his fingers through his hair. "Stand down," he said. After his agents complied, the two detectives put their guns away.

"This is my scene." Epps looked at his watch. "It's been my scene for twelve minutes. Your boss and the local chief just got the paperwork. You can call Inspector Zinn now or check when you're back at your precinct."

Salerno went to the phone and beeped his boss, who called him back in moments, "He's right, Jimmy. I got the paperwork not five minutes ago. It came from Downtown."

"Fuck me."

"Fuck us all, Jimmy."

"The brother's here," Salerno told his boss in code. "Says he did what he told you."

Epps reached for the phone, but Salerno hung it up.

"I'll take everything you and your partner got, Detective. You hold anything back, you're obstructing justice." He turned to Lucas Rook. "Seems to me if that shield is real, you're way out of your jurisdiction. You got some questions to answer. Maybe some hard ones."

"He's with us," Salerno lied. "Tasked down from NYPD. It'll all be in the case file. You'll have that in an hour."

The ASAC was pleased with the compliance. "Very good," he answered. "Now how about you vacate my crime scene." He smoothed the shock of red hair from off his forehead.

The three of them headed for the front door, Chick keeping Rook between himself and Salerno. The agent at the door was slow to move out of the way. She was an intense woman with straight blonde hair.

"How about it, Missy?" Jimmy said.

Agent Dellum motioned for Handler to let them through.

"Fucking fuckers always got to take it over," Salerno said when they got outside.

"They fuck it all up," Chick said.

Rook started towards his car, but Salerno stopped him.

"You too, New York, and we're taking you in," he said.

Misher brought out his blackjack. Rook set himself and brought his out. "I'll give you as good as I get."

Salerno moved in, but saw Epps and Dellum coming out to their car. "This don't look right. I'll ride back with you, Rook," Jimmy said. "We'll straighten this out soon enough."

"You alright, partner?" Chick asked him.

Salerno nodded and followed Rook over to his car.

26

There was no talk as Rook and Salerno drove back to the station. It had gotten cold, and Jimmy turned the heater on. The air smelled like burning metal.

Misher followed close in so that his partner didn't have to check the rear view. Chick checked his own mirror to make sure that the Feds weren't following them in.

Salerno spoke to Rook for the first time as they pulled up to the precinct, "You going to give me what you got or we going to jam you up?"

"You get it all at Joe Zinn's desk. You want to tell him it's yours, you tell him any story you want."

Misher pulled alongside and got out first. He could see Rook reaching over the seat for his cane and reached in his jacket to get out his gun. "Leave the stick," he said.

"You think I got a sword in there?"

"I've seen that before."

"Well, not this time, friend. This ain't the movies."

Jimmy got out as his partner came around to the passenger's side. They walked over to the back entrance with Rook, not like they were bringing him in, but not like he was one of them either.

Joe Garrett was coming out as they were going. He was still wearing his blues, but he was on the way home.

"Good shift?" Rook asked him.

"Another step towards fame and fortune," Garrett answered as he walked by.

"Don't say nothing to no one, New York," Misher said. "This is our house, not the fucking Waldorf Astoria."

Salerno nodded in agreement to his partner, and the two of them ushered Rook into the precinct. The night's collars were still there and some of the blues that brought them in were there lounging around waiting for them to be processed. When the three got upstairs, Inspector Zinn's blinds were drawn. Misher pointed to the metal desk that Lefko had been used. "Sit and don't touch nothing," he told Rook.

Jimmy knocked on the door twice. When the Inspector did not respond, he went back to his desk. There was a sheaf of pink message slips on his desk. He worked them, keeping an eye on Rook, who asked, "How do I get an outside line?"

"You don't," Misher answered.

Rook smiled. He opened the bottom drawer of the green desk and stretched his bad leg across it. "You two are a piece of work."

Misher wasn't going to let that go, but Joe Zinn opened his door. "Detectives," he said. He wasn't smiling.

"Not you, New York," Salerno added. "And don't touch nothing."

Once they were inside the office, Rook began copying down the notes and bits of information on the desk blotter and calendar.

"Jesus Christ!" Zinn said when his glass door was closed again. "What a cluster fuck!"

172

"What's up?" Chick asked.

"What's up? I'll tell you what's up." The Inspector rearranged the cushion on his seat. "I've been trying to get a decent desk chair for two years. You're killing me, that's what's up. I've got three calls in the last half hour. No, four, if you count Ed Goodstein's because I hung up on him when he told me to go fuck myself. He's fuming because you didn't give him the courtesy of a 'heads up' that you were coming in.

"Then, of course, Epps wants to know if I'm going to like my retirement because of the lack of cooperation we're giving and that we're going to get a call from the Chief's office which, of course, I get in the next two minutes. You don't want to guess what that was like. You two cowboys want to tell me what's going on?" Inspector Zinn got up and then sat back down again and began rummaging through his desk.

"You want Advils, boss?"

"I don't want no Advils, Chick. They make my ass bleed. What I do want to know is what's going on."

Detective Salerno reached to straighten the clip-on tie he wore for meetings. but realized he had forgotten it. "It was that New York prick. You told us the job was the Feds'. It's the Feds. We're not putting you in the middle of nothing, boss."

"We see this Rook sniffing around," Misher said. "Acting all hinky and all. We do our job. We follow the guy. We know he's private and he can mess things up for the Department. My partner and me both called Chief Goodstein, but they said he was in some meeting or whatever. A lot of 'two's' in that office, not that the African-American woman who took my message wasn't very nice and all."

"This Rook guy, we brought him in. He leads us to Stewart Charles Dunmoore except that he's very dead. I get a thread from one of the little rug steps the piano teacher had his kids put their feet on so they can reach the piano where he's giving his lessons now or whatever. No way it don't match the one we took off the dead girl. Then the college boys show up and we're happy to leave Rook with them, but he says he broke the case and it's all yours. I told the Feebs he's tasked over to us so they'd give me the opportunity to bring Rook back into our house."

"We got a circus here, gentlemen. Downtown, the Feds, the papers, this PI. Even one of them supermarket rags called. Let's see what Rook has. He wants to be in the middle of things, I just might accommodate him."

Misher brought Rook into the Inspector's office. Even with the limp, he walked like a cop.

Zinn offered no pleasantries. "What do you got and what were you doing at a crime scene?"

"We're doing this on our understanding, Inspector. I give over what I got to you. Then I call my client. He's the first to know outside of this room."

"Agreed," Zinn answered.

Rook took off his coat and unzipped the lining. Salerno and Misher watched his every move. Inside the lining was a plastic bread bag that contained a folded piece of paper.

"You fold it?"

"I bagged it up, Detective."

Zinn put a piece of clean white paper on his desk and took the note out with the blunt end of two pens that he held like chopsticks. It was musical score paper. The Inspector read it.

"My call?"

"I think you should wait, Rook," Zinn told him.

"Read the note, boss," Salerno said.

"'I cannot go on. I am responsible for the death of a child.'"

"So?" Rook said.

"So?" Inspector Zinn answered. "What you got don't solve a thing. We got more than one dead kid."

The Inspector plugged his teapot in. "My Department is going to be eaten-up by this, Rook," he said. "The Feebs are here to the rescue. And I can't use any of my people. We're going to look like a bunch of dummies and the bad guys will get the scent." He poured himself a cup of lukewarm tea.

Joe Zinn nodded subtly to Salerno and Chick as he told Rook of the other dead girls. The detectives knew what was going on, that the boss was putting Rook in the middle of the bag of shit. The outsider would be where he belonged.

27

Rook left Joe Zinn's office knowing that everybody would be using everybody else. He was halfway across the squad room when Detective Lefko came in. Gene wore a tan trench coat and gray Jeff-cap and smelled like cigars. Rook watched him drop his hat and gloves, then slide the pile away to jot something on the desk blotter before going to the Inspector's office.

Lieutenant Esposito was next. Rook said "Good evening" as she passed by with her fine ass.

The final members of his Task Force present, Zinn closed the blinds in his glass-enclosed office. This gave Rook the opportunity to check what Lefko had written. It read: "bread, milk, and yellow onions," the long arm of domesticity. But it gave Rook the opportunity to check the handwriting against the others on the blotter. There were four matches: a long distance phone number, which he recognized to be Rochester, New York, another grocery order and the home address of Donald Jelks.

Inside Joe Zinn's office, Lefko was confirming that he was stand-up, "This ain't right, Inspector. You're on a case and then the politics takes you off of it. They're ruining the job." He turned in his chair. "Especially for you, Jimmy. It's your case. Yours and Chick's. Them Feds should stay in Washington where they belong."

The Inspector nodded. "We appreciate that, Gene, so you'll turn in your dailys, notes, whatever."

"The college boys, that girl, Agent Handler whatever, already asked me for them, Inspector." He paused only slightly, but it was enough for Salerno to tighten up. Lefko went on, "I told her I lost it all, left my paperwork somewhere or other. Handler asked me for a copy of my disk for which I told her we were still in the 70's, but if I turned up anything, I'd be glad to pass it on."

"Like the kidney stone you had last year."

"Don't even remind me, Chick. I don't even want to be thinking of that."

"If you could remember anything, which you can't, Gene, what would it be you couldn't remember?" Salerno asked.

Lefko shook his head. "I came up with squat if you're talking anything I give the Feebs, Jimmy. But for in here, Mr. Jeltz was on business in Rochester, New York, and no way is he able to come back here, do his kid, then get back to Rochester to fly back here. No way."

The detective liked being center stage and made the best of it. "Before you had to pull me off, I had Q&A'd the mother. She's fried, but other than that there's no indication she's involved. I couldn't find nothing about piano lessons like Jimmy asked me. The only other thing, they had their oil burner serviced, and I went to Q&A him. On the other hand…"

"Is there a short version, Gene?" Zinn asked.

"The short version, Inspector, is I like the mother anyway."

"Even though you just said she's clean?"

"Let me tell you why," Lefko answered, taking out his notebook. "There's this neighbor."

"Rose Colanzi," the Inspector added.

"I don't mean her. In the back, Inspector, where the lawn slopes down to the woods." He turned to Salerno. "You wanted to know the name of who Colzani works for, Jimmy. I asked her. Mark Braslow. He's a podiatrist. No forgive in that woman. I mention Donald, the father, she gets all wired about him being out of town."

He turned back to the Inspector. "This social worker lives in the back." He consulted his note pad again. "With fourteen cats, Jacqueline Coulter. The lady had like a glass eye. It's like it's looking at you, and it isn't. Do you believe that?"

Salerno was agitated about the lack of direct connection to the thread and Dunmoore since the Jelk's girl didn't take piano lessons. He twirled a pencil in his fingers. "Fourteen cats you say, Gene?"

"Right, fourteen, Jimmy. She tells me she's not supposed to say anything even though she's not doing any social work stuff for the family. But she goes ahead anyway."

"With what, Detective?"

"She says the father is away way too much, boss. That maybe Mrs. Jeltz is trying to get his attention."

"By killing their kid?" Esposito asked him.

"She said, the cat lady did, that she thought the second kid was Mr. Jeltz' idea." He looked at his notes. "She told me to read this book called *Death of Innocents*. I worked her pretty good, Inspector. I don't have anything else, but my gut tells me it's the mother."

The Inspector looked at Esposito, who had her hand partly raised. "From what I've been reading, boss, Samuel's book

178

about post partum murders, the second kid's too old for that. Although I can see her hating her husband, being afraid of him so she takes it out on her daughter."

Zinn didn't follow that. He stood up which meant the meeting was over. "Thank you for your help, people. This concludes the debrief of our Task Force. Detective Lefko, I know you want to get back to your house. I'll see that your personnel jacket will appropriately reflect your help here."

"Good working with you, Inspector. It's been my pleasure, a real highlight, I mean." Lefko started to put on his trench coat and then stopped to add, "And you two guys," and then "And you, too, Esposito."

"Keep on dancing," Chick told him.

Detective Lefko left without shaking hands. Some cops didn't shake hands, like they knew they had something bad to pass on.

The Inspector told Esposito that he appreciated her assistance too. She knew that was her signal and she closed the glass door behind her.

The two detectives sat there.

"Maybe we got an indirect transfer of the piano man's carpet thread boss. Maybe another vic takes it with them, and the Jelks' girl picks it up."

"It's the Bureau's case now, Jimmy," the Inspector said. "Any investigation of a Locard's Principle Exchange is going to have to be by the Feds."

"In a pig's eye," Salerno answered. "I'm out and you let that bottom-feeding New York gimp in."

The Inspector didn't like that Salerno was getting in his face, but he understood the motivation. He took a deep breath. "Rook's a roll of paper if shit gets out of the bag. That's what he is." Inspector Zinn paused and counted to five. "This is the Fed's case now, Salerno. Stay out of it."

Salerno's clenched his teeth. He was about to respond, but his partner cut him off. "He will, boss, he will."

It had raped her heart, poisoned her mind. She was insane, living in a world no one saw, seeing things that no one had even seen. There were noises in her brain.

She felt strong and whole when she grabbed them up and did the things she did. Her face was bright.

The pile of the little girl's clothes lay like a puddle at her feet. It was a good thing she was doing now. Keeping them in the soft white robes. She heard sounds roaring in her head fifty years ago. The beating of wings, thousands of them. The sky black with them. Her eyes became a reptile's as she went into the other room where the child slept in her soft, white robe, with shiny hair like a broken wing on the clean white sheets.

The killer of innocent children smelled the air. "No one is safe," she said out loud, and she fell upon the child like an axe.

28

At eight thirty that morning, Assistant Special Agent Robert Epps was trying his best to have his take-over run smoothly. "We appreciate the opportunity to work with you, Inspector." He introduced Dellum and Agent Handler.

Zinn shock hands.

Epps smiled. "First, we'd like to go over whatever you have on the Jelks case. Field reports, anything from the scene, the autopsy report. We'll work closely, of course, with whomever you designate, Joe."

The Inspector nodded.

"Agents Dellum and Handler would like to sit down with your Lead on this job. Also on any other similar cases."

"I specialize in geographical cross-references and time lines," Handler added.

"Is that right?" the Inspector asked.

Epps smoothed his red hair off his forehead. "Give the Inspector and me a minute, people," he told his agents. They stepped out, and he spoke immediately, "We'll absolutely protect your command authority. I guarantee it."

"That's not enough." Zinn was irritated and it showed.

"What's not enough, Inspector?"

"I got the integrity of this precinct to think about. I got my people to think about. This has got to be a joint investigation."

The ASAC stood up. "Inspector, you can have someone act as liaison. You can call it whatever you need to, but they're only liasing. I think the directives from your Chief's office were quite clear."

Zinn knew that taking it any further at this time was futile. He picked up his intercom. "Esposito, our guests are here."

She was there in moments, passing the woman and her partner who waited outside the Inspector's office. Zinn introduced her as she arrived. "Assistant Special Agent Epps, this is our Information Officer. She'll be happy to bring your people up to speed."

The ASAC smiled again. "It will be a pleasure working with you, I'm sure, Lieutenant." Then Epps turned back to Joe Zinn. "Let's set up that meeting with your Lead as soon as possible. Salerno, isn't it?"

"He is."

"I appreciate your cooperation, Joe. It will certainly be reflected in my report."

Zinn started shuffling papers on his desk. "Esposito, our guests will need a place to work out of for the time they're here. You can show them to the new conference room on the first level."

She looked at him.

"Use the steps to the right of the parking lot entrance," he told her.

The IO smiled, realizing that her boss was referring to the basement. It had to be a zillion degrees down there. She went out and introduced herself to the two agents.

Eileen Handler tried to hold her gaze, but Esposito turned to Dellum. "I saw you play in college. You could really bring it."

"You a big sports fan?" Dellum asked. He had long ago tired of explaining that all big black men didn't play football or basketball. In fact, sports did not interest him at all. He smiled. "If you can show us to our work area, we'd like to set up. We have an appointment in less than an hour, and we keep to our schedule."

"Do you need me to coordinate anything for you?" she asked.

"We're going to meet with your Medical Examiner. You're welcome to join us," Dellum offered.

"I've got to pass," she answered. "Listen, to save time, Agent Handler could check out the new conference room while I show you our house."

"Think that will give you two enough time?" Handler said under her breath.

Vanessa started up the steps so Dellum could get a good look at her. When they got to the landing, she leaned against the wall.

"You comin' on to me, Lieutenant Esposito?"

"It depends on how I'm doing." She opened the door and went inside. "Excuse me for a minute," Esposito told him. "I've got to powder my nose."

Down the hall was the bullpen where the Robbery and Civil Disobedience squads sat. She grabbed a phone and buzzed the Inspector, who was just putting on his running shoes.

"Boss, they're going out to see Doc Nessel. I thought you'd want to know."

"Right, right. Good job," he told her.

Zinn hung up and called the Medical Examiner.

The secretary put him on hold. "I'm sorry, Dr. Nessel is occupied."

"That's nice, dear. You put him on now. Your job depends on it."

Nessel picked up the phone in a matter of moments.

"I hope your patient doesn't mind the interruption, Sam," the Inspector said.

"What is it, Joe? I've got work to do."

"The Feds are on the way over to see you. They'll be there in twenty minutes." He could hear the M.E. light a cigarette.

"I don't have anything to hide, Joe."

Zinn was torn between getting a better look at what Nessel had on the dead girls and doing anything that could be considered as obstructing the Bureau's investigation. "That's up to you. I don't know what you have and what you don't. And I'm not telling you not to talk to them or what to say. I just thought you might want to compose yourself first."

"I haven't been feeling too well."

The Inspector thought of taking him to the cop bar. Remind him whose side he was on. "Maybe we can grab a beer sometime at Bill Higgins' place on the Boulevard."

The M.E started to hang up but then added, "This conversation never happened, Joe."

"What a jerk-off," Zinn said as he went out. He set out at a brisk, steady pace, wanting to break into a trot. Whenever possible he stayed on the grass because the jarring was bad for his hemorrhoids. The run cleared his mind. When he got back to the house, he went in through the precinct's front door.

"Everything in order?" he asked the desk sergeant.

"Our guests aren't too happy in the new conference room," Joe Garrett answered.

"We do our best, Sergeant. We do our best. Any activity?"

"Not to speak of, boss. Radicchio took a call off the alarm from the coin shop up on the avenue which turned out to be some kids. He called juvy."

"Have an easy shift," the Inspector said and went upstairs. After he cleaned-up and changed clothes, Zinn called his Information Officer. "Everything under control?" he asked her.

"It is, boss. And the ASAC hasn't been back yet."

"Any questions or problems, come to me, Lieutenant."

"I can handle this, Inspector, but I certainly will."

Joe Zinn hung up and checked his voice mail. His wife had called about taking their neighbor to the dentist. There was a call from Downtown, from the Deputy Chief's Office. They could kiss his Sunday ass now that they turned the Jelk's case over to the Feds. And Nessel called. "You liked the angels" was the only message he left.

"The angels" meant Sam's garage. Meet him in his garage, the paranoid midget sack of crap. Probably thinks the Feds got his phone tapped. If he only knew how rare that kind of stuff really was. Or was the M.E. worried about something particular. Maybe he had something to hide.

Zinn drove over to see Nessel and find out.

The City Avenue bridge was closed again, so he took the West River Drive. He drove behind the Adams Mark Hotel and through Wynnefield so he could avoid City Line, which was always a mess. Presidential Boulevard was faster, but that was Montgomery County and, even though he got reciprocity in the surrounding counties, the Inspector stayed in his own territory as much as he could.

Joe Zinn pushed his driving. It was probably only because the FBI was coming to see him that Nessel was willing to talk. No way would Zinn obstruct the Feds' investigation, but he wanted what Sam had to give.

Virginia Nessel was just coming back from walking their Bouvier when the Inspector pulled up. The dog strained at the leash and barked.

"He just wants to play." Then she realized who it was. "I recognized you this time, Inspector. Let me get him into the house."

Zinn parked in the driveway. The Cadillac was not in sight. He walked over to the garage which served as Nessel's wood shop. "Sam, it's Joe Zinn," he called and then knocked on the door. There was no answer, and he couldn't hear any machines running.

Zinn walked around to the front of the house and rang the bell.

Mrs. Nessel opened the door. "I wondered where you went," she said "Sam said to tell you he's taking you up on your invitation. That you'll know what he means."

"Sure, Virginia. Nice to see you again. Handsome dog. Bouvier, isn't?"

She smiled and stood with the door open a little too long. He figured she probably wanted him to either talk about how odd her husband had been acting or for him to haul her ashes. He didn't care in either case. Zinn went to Bill Higgins' place, annoyed by the M.E.'s cloak-and-dagger stuff and the waste of gas.

Sam Nessel sat the bar staring at the sign, "It's Us Against Them". He was a tiny man, slightly larger than a dwarf and he looked silly on the stool.

Young Billy Higgins was trying bar talk, "How about 'Pat the Bat'? Another Mark McGuire, huh?"

The Medical Eexaminer didn't answer and lit another cigarette. Two black detectives came in for cold ones and sat in the front booth. A blind woman opened the door, but turned around and left. Nessel looked at his watch.

Zinn came in and walked over to the bar. "Sam, you want to take a booth?"

"What'll you have?" young Billy asked.

The Inspector looked at him. "You're Bill Higgins' boy. You favor him."

"Injured on Duty. Fell off a roof at the One-Five."

"The Fifteenth, they run a good house," the Inspector said. "That's Clarence Rutty's precinct. He's a good man."

"Yes he is…"

"Tell your Dad that Joe Zinn was asking for him. Haven't been here in a couple of years. Sorry about your mother."

The Inspector took Nessel to the booth in the back. He could see that the M.E. was shaken up. It could be he was just scared at being talked to by the Feds. Most people were.

Sam reached for his smokes, but realized he had left them on the bar with his drink. He started to get up, but the Inspector gestured for him to sit down. "Christ, Joe, we got to go through this again? You thinking that I stole the cranial saw or climbed on one of my patients or whatever?"

The Inspector didn't answer. Then after along pause, he said, "You want to tell me about it, Sam?"

The little man fiddled with the silverware. "Tell you what?"

"You called me, Doc. The only way I can help you is if you fill me in on the details."

Nessel slid out of the booth and went over to the bar, walking self-consciously the way he did in open spaces. He lit a cigarette and finished his Jack Daniels. The alcohol fortified Sam, and he thought about leaving, taking his chances, call his lawyer, not that he had anything really to worry about even if Zinn was "working him." He had been around cops long enough to know that the Inspector was fishing. The M.E. went back to their table.

"I appreciate your meeting me, Joe. I do. I feel better. You know I've got it in perspective now. Just your meeting with me, you know, having a drink together." Nessel made a clumsy gesture of looking at his watch.

"Sure, Doc. If that's the way you want to leave this, the Feds coming to see you. It's good you feel okay because they will be pretty rough. If you change your mind or anything, give me a call." When they shook hands, Inspector Zinn was surprised by the strength of his grip.

Samuel P. Nessel, M.D., the esteemed Medical Examiner, felt in control as he left. But as he drove along he began to unravel again, more and more—like someone was pulling on a loose end that would leave him all undone.

Little Molly Hearn lay in a clean, white robe, her body turning cold. The killer lay next to her. The right thing had been done. A child had been saved from harm, from horrible things. The words flew around the room and hung in the air, "Down came a blackbird and pecked off her nose." And the slayer of little girls fell asleep, inhaling the scents of life and death.

29

Jimmy and Chick sat in the back of Marge's. The place was freshly painted, but with the old colors, battleship gray and dark blue woodwork.

"You think we did wrong when we stopped coming over here when the Dunkin Donuts opened?"

"It just happened, Chick. Marge had the stroke and they were closed more than a month." Jimmy finished his cup and held it up for a refill.

The waitress came over. She was half-Asian, half black with green eyes and smelled of sandalwood.

"You got my partner's signal, Miss?" Chick wanted her to know he was a cop. "And you'll excuse me if I tell you in my unofficial capacity that you smell great. And what beautiful opal eyes you have. I'm Detective Misher."

"My name is Serena," she answered, "and…"

"You can call me Chick over a glass of wine."

"Excuse me," she answered. "Did you just ask me out?" She walked away without shaking her ass even a little bit.

"That's not a 'yes,' partner," Jimmy shook his head. "Don't even think about it."

"I can't help thinking about it. I'm sitting here with a friggin' tent in my pants."

Salerno took his napkin and wiped away a wet spot on the table. "The boss says I'm supposed to meet the Feebs today, partner. Maybe you want to take some lost time so you don't get caught up in the shit storm."

"You going to talk to them college boys, Jimmy?"

"The boss says I got to meet with them, I got to meet with them." He sipped his coffee. "They don't know what a mute prick I am."

"What about the Raimondo case if they ask, Jimmy?"

"My amnesia comes back, whatever."

Serena brought back their eggs and toast. "I hope everything's to your liking, Detectives."

"It's perfect, just perfect," Misher answered. "Would you marry me or at least let me buy you that glass of white wine?"

She blushed.

"Paint you toenails?" he asked.

"I'm seventeen."

"Of course you are, dear," Chick told her as she left again. "I'm a dead man, James, a dead man. She's shaking her booty at me, and I'm old enough to be her father."

Salerno's egges were scrambled well, the way he liked them. "Grab me the mustard, will you, partner?" he asked. "That is, if the teen hop is over."

Chick reached over to the table behind him. "I can never get over that, Jimmy, mustard on eggs. Ketchup maybe. Mayo on french fries. I had that once."

"Jack O'Meara used to put mayo on everything."

"Or Johnnie Walker." Misher waited until Salerno had eaten the last forkful of scrambled eggs with the last bite of toast. "What do you do they ask you about the evidence you got off the vic when I was in the barbecue joint?"

Salerno took the napkin out of his shirt. "I got nothing to tell them. Everything I may have got, if I got anything, I turned in. So I got nothing for them."

"Good, Jimmy, good." Chick held up his cup for another refill. "I got to keep drinking this stuff until my green-eyed angel comes of age."

When Zinn got back to his precinct from meeting with Nessel, his deskman was involved in a heated argument with Agents Handler and Dellum, "Nobody told me nothing about nobody going downstairs. Like I told you, you'll have to wait for the Inspector."

The front phone rang. As Dellum had threatened, it was Assistant Special Agent in Charge Robert Epps. The deskman looked over and saw the Inspector. "I think it's for you, boss. Somebody from the Bureau is giving me an earful."

Zinn took the receiver. "Just logistics, Bob," he said "My people aren't used to yours. Our federal guests are always welcome," he said as he hung up.

"We need to talk to your Lead," Dellum told the Inspector. "Our ASAC said he cleared that with you."

"Detective Salerno," Handler added.

"Thank you, Agent Handler. I know who my people are. Why don't you two get set up." He started to the stairs. "I'll check the schedule. See who took vacation or whatever."

"That's bullshit, Inspector."

The Inspector turned around. "Look, Miss Handler, I don't know how long you've been in the field so I'm giving you the benefit of the doubt, but any more of that and you and Dellum here are out of here no matter who says what."

Dellum put his hand on his partner's arm. "I'll see you downstairs in a minute."

"I got to get out of here, R.D.." she added quietly. "The oven they got us in is killing me. I'll see you outside."

"Like I said, Renaldo," the Inspector said. "Let me check the schedule. There's no nonsense here. I'll check on my detective's availability and see to it that this gets done."

Dellum met his partner in front of the precinct where she was grabbing a smoke. "This is childish bullshit," Handler said. "I expect this from my twelve year old, not a police inspector."

"We're not going anywhere, Eileen," he answered. "In fact, we're going to sit on the elusive Detective Salerno."

They parked in the alley across the street from the entrance to the precinct parking lot. The agents waited for an hour for Salerno, "I could use a cup of coffee," Dellum said.

"There's a Dunkin Donuts' around the block," she said. "Let's give it another fifteen minutes, although my guess is he isn't coming in."

It was Chick Misher's turn to drive as they left breakfast. He took his own route back to the precinct, which included a wrong way trip down Buttonwood Street.

"No doubt we'll be going to that place regularly," Jimmy said, "now that you're in love. But no way you tell me your route is two minutes better. You're going down a one way voids it."

As they came down Buttonwood, Chick made the two FBI agents parked in the alley. "Probably waiting on us, partner."

He made two rights and went down another one way street to come to their precinct house.

"Unless they're giving each other hand jobs, Chick. Who do you think got the bigger dick?"

"Definitely Handler, Jimmy. Definitely."

Misher made another observation as the detectives pulled into the parking lot, "Seems we got a mystery guest. We got the M.E. parked in the shadows over there with his hat pulled down over his face."

"How do you know it's Nessel?"

"His Cadillac has a sign in the back window, Jimmy. Says 'Official Business-City Medical Examiner'."

"You're a real Sherlock Holmes, Chick."

"I dress better," Misher told him.

30

The two detectives waited in the garage, eyeing up Sam Nessel. Misher started pushing back his cuticles with the file he had taken from his lock set. "You want to sit on him, Jimmy, or we go up to the squad?

"Sit on him, Chick, the way he's being all in the shadows, something's up." Salerno slid the seat all the way back. "I got him."

"You want me to bring you a cup from the coffee room, Jimmy?"

"You trying to kill me, partner?"

Misher opened the car door. "No, I meant you going to be sitting on this guy a while and you might want a piss jar."

"Check my messages, will you, Chick?"

Misher went up the back steps. Esposito was coming down. He saw her legs first and then how her uniform blouse was as usual, too tight. "You sneaking around?"

"Right," Vanessa answered. "We got to stop meeting like this."

"In my dreams," Chick said smiling. He shook his head and went upstairs. There were pink slips on his phone and his partner's, including one for each of them from Lucas Rook.

Detective Misher knocked on the Inspector's glass door. Zinn was going through a stack of 61's and waved him in.

"What's up?" he asked.

"Doc Nessel's parking in the garage. Over in the shadows. Got his hat pulled down and all. Jimmy's sitting on him. You want us to bring him up or what?"

"He's supposed to meet with the Eyes, like your partner. Sam's getting his nerve up to come talk to me about it."

"They're sitting on our house. Me and Jimmy made them college girls sitting in the alley on our way in."

"I don't like them around our house. Not a bit." The Inspector took a deep breath and let it out slowly. "These Feds are better than most, especially for what they're sniffing around here for. Epps tells me he worked the Polly Klass job in '93 and the Atlanta serial thing, although I doubt he was on both. These two aren't right, though, eyeballing our house. Epps is going to hear from me about this."

Zinn reached over to the small table behind him and felt the electric tea pot. "You want a cup?"

"I'm not really a tea man, boss. It gets my stomach pretty good."

"I got herbal."

Misher realized that the Inspector was going somewhere with the small talk and that running would only make it worse. "Sure, boss, sure. You got honey to go with that?"

Zinn brought out a plastic bear from his desk drawer. "Honey it is." He poured the cups and then went on. "I don't like the Feebs around here. Not at all. But they got a lot of resources. At least that's one of the main 'reasons' Downtown gives me that they got jurisdiction, like that they're going to laser the whole house. Going to run everybody through NCIC. Jelks, the neighbors, whatever. Check to see whether there were other jobs elsewhere that fit the profile."

"Jelks was up in New York State when it went down."

Zinn sipped his tea. "Mine's just warm. This pot's about had it. Yours alright?"

"Fine, Inspector, fine. They going to put him on the box?"

"They get a reason to polygraph Jelks, they'll wire him up in a second, even though that's our job."

Chick put his cup down. "All well and good, Inspector, that scientific shit, but it's police work that clears cases. BSU, they going to send 'Bullshit University' too, right?"

"You got that, Chick. Behavioral Sciences is on the way."

"It's police work, reworking the leads and all that's going to clear this shit pile, boss."

The Inspector felt the tea pot again. "Jimmy alright?"

"My partner's always alright, boss."

Zinn realized it probably hadn't come out right and that maybe he shouldn't have been taking that tack at all. He tried to go ahead and fix it. "I meant with the Feebs, Chick. He's going to have to work with them. Epps is pressing me."

"With respect, boss, I'm not having any conversation about my partner."

Joe didn't like the tone, but he let it pass. "About the M.E., flush him out, will you, Chick. I don't got all day. And we don't want Sam Nessel offing himself on our property."

Misher went back down into the garage and motioned his partner to join him. Even though there was no reason to expect any trouble, the two of them approached the Medical Examiner's Cadillac as if they were making a traffic stop. Salerno came up to the driver's side and his partner to the passenger's. Both had their jackets open so that they could reach their weapons.

Sam Nessel had the front seat up high so he could see out the windshield. His head and hands were resting on the steering wheel. The car was filled with cigarette smoke. Salerno knocked on the car window. "Open the door, Doc," he said. "It looks like the Chicago fire in there."

Chick tried the passenger door. It was open. "Second-hand smoke's hazardous to your health," he said.

The Medical Examiner lifted up his head. His face was pale and clammy. "I'm not feeling well," he answered.

"I wouldn't think so. Here, let me give you a hand."

"I'm good, Salerno. I'm good."

"You don't look too good, Doc," Chick told him.

The M.E. lit another cigarette and got out of his car. "I'm here to see Joe Zinn," he said. "We go back a long time." He brushed the ashes off his sport jacket.

"Right," Misher replied. "He's a good man. We're going upstairs. We'll walk with you. Maybe you got some good autopsy stories."

The Medical Examiner particularly did not like the way he looked and felt walking in a group. He took a double hit of the menthol smoke. When they were inside, Chick asked Jimmy to take Nessel over to the boss, "I got some calls to make, partner," he said. He had enough of Joe Zinn for one morning.

The Inspector was going over requests for overtime when Salerno knocked on the door. Nessel had tried to compose himself, but was patting the pocket where he kept his cigarettes. Salerno threw a half-salute to the Inspector and went back to the squad.

Zinn wanted the Medical Examiner on edge. "Sorry, it's a smoke-free building, Sam."

"Excuse me?"

"You were reaching for your smokes."

"Habit, Joe, habit."

"Sure. What can I do for you?" He gestured to the chair in front of him.

"Your people brought me up here, Joe."

The Inspector let that go and went right at him. "You speak to the Feds yet, Sam? That'd knock anybody off kilter. They can be pretty rough." He could see Nessel twitch. "You want a cup of coffee? We can go down to the coffee room."

"Good, Joe."

They walked down the green hall to the windowless room, Zinn walking slow so that the M.E's small strides could keep pace. Detective Muldoon was playing solitaire, but left his cards when he saw the boss come in.

Zinn poured a cup for Nessel and sat across from him at the metal table. "Tell me about it, Sam. Tell me. That's why you're here."

"It made sense, what you told me out at the house, Joe. You know about the FBI and all."

"Right." The Inspector sat with his hands folded in front of him.

"You know. And that I could talk to you first."

"Why's that, Sam?"

"Not that I've got anything to hide, mind you. But like you said, Joe, the Feds…"

The Inspector started to get up. "I got things to do, Sam. You got something to say, you want my help, talk to me now. You want to wait for the Feds, that's alright with me. They're parked across the street. Two agents have been following you."

"They'll find out. There's no way I can hide it any more." Tears started down Nessel's face, and he reached for a napkin to wipe them away. He started to shake his head and covered his face with his stubby hands.

"You tell me now, Sam. Tell me now or I'll have the Federal Government in here in thirty seconds. They got that mandatory sentencing. The next time you'll see your wife again you'll be an old, old man." Inspector Zinn paused for effect. "You'll be ruined."

"Virginia," Nessel wept. He took a cigarette out of his pocket, but the Inspector knocked it away and reached for the phone.

Nessel wiped his face again. "They'll be able to tell," he said. "They'll be able to tell. I tried to leave them alone. Then it got easier and easier as I went along. I knew it was crazy. Like in a dream. Like something was pulling me on. And somehow that nobody would ever know." The Medical Examiner stopped.

Inspector Zinn waited for him, then started to reach for the phone again.

"Look at me, Joe. Just look at me. I know what I am. I'm not even five feet tall. I'm a freak, I know that. But I'm no monster. I tried to keave them so they were alright."

"What about their parents? What about Heather Raimondo?"

"Not her. Not her." Nessel reached for a cigarette. Zinn let him light it. "The others like her. How do you think I stayed so busy. Sometimes both rooms backed up," the Medical Examiner said through a cloud of smoke. "All of the overtime, the budget, the personnel. I was The Man."

Inspector Zinn got out of his chair and placed himself between the M.E. and the door. "I'll get the video recorder in here. We'll get it down on tape. It will be all over. I'll help you, Sam. We'll get it down to manslaughter, second degree, maybe involuntary. We'll keep it quiet. You'll get consideration, being you're a doctor and all."

The Medical Examiner's face turned ashen. "No! No!" he shouted. "Jesus, Joe. No. No! They were already dead. The numbers...the numbers. That's all I did. I moved the bodies around. Sometimes I did cases more than once. I cut them open twice. That's all, Joe. That's all. I'm going to be alright, aren't I?"

The Inspector was furious. He understood that Dr. Samuel Nessel was a ghoul and not a murderer. "You're pathetic," he said.

"I'll be alright, Joe, right? I pay my taxes. I'm trying to get it right...working in a clinic, doing charity work."

"Who gives a shit, Sam? I've got better things to do." Zinn buzzed Detective Misher to come in and take the M.E.'s statement.

31

Chick was out at Marge's when the Inspector called for him. When he got back to the precinct, he went to the coffee room. Salerno was there with Muldoon.

Misher put the bags on the table.

"The boss wants you to take Nessel's statement," Jimmy told him. "Just chicken shit. He thought the M.E. was copping to the kid homicides, but it's just chicken shit. The boss'll fill you in. The Mississippi gambler here will run the tape. I got to sit down with the Eyes. The boss says I can't dodge them any more."

Muldoon wiped the custard away from the corner of his mouth. "Empty suits."

"You got that right," Misher said.

Salerno left the coffee room with his tea and cruller in his left hand. He went down the backstairs into the basement, passing by the sweltering space next to the boiler room that Zinn had delegated for the FBI office.

There was a side door that allowed the detective to leave out of view of the two Feebs still sitting in the alley across from the station house. The building next door to the precinct had been closed for sometime. Two years ago, Russian entrepreneurs tried to get a sweat shop going before Licenses and Inspections shut them down.

The present owners, who hoped that the closeness of the police precinct would entice a developer, had recently installed new doors and locks. Detective Salerno took out his pick kit and was inside in moments. He went out the back door and around behind the immaculate dark blue sedan that held the two FBI agents.

Dellum was reading a newspaper. Agent Handler had her eyes on the station house. It was easy for Jimmy to come up on the big Mercury. He knocked on the driver's side window.

Renaldo Dellum folded his paper. "Detective Salerno, isn't it?"

Jimmy looked at him without a word.

"Your first name's Jim, James, right?" the agent repeated. He offered his large hand through the open car window. "My friends call me 'RD'."

"You can call me 'Detective'," Salerno answered.

Handler turned to him "How about 'patrolman'? We can arrange that."

"Easy," Renaldo put his hand on her arm.

Salerno leaned against the brick wall behind him and looked at his watch, "I'm giving this whole thing twenty minutes, including coming across the street. So if you want to talk to me, Dellum, you'd better get at it."

"Fine, Detective. You want to adjourn to your building, that's fine. If not, we could grab a cup of coffee or you could follow me back to our office."

"I know a place. I'll be around front in two minutes. That will be time enough to dispose of Cagney and Lacey here. I'm supposed to talk to you, I talk to you. You want me to talk to her, I'll talk to her while you go shoot some hoops."

"You are an asshole, Salerno."

"That comes with the territory, Agent Dellum." Salerno walked away.

Handler wanted in on the meeting, but Dellum told her otherwise, "I understand that protocol dictates that we both conduct the interview so we're each a corroborating witness for the other, but that's not going to work with him, Eileen. He's been around too long. Besides, unlike me, I don't think he likes you."

"Great loss." Handler took out a cigarette, waiting to light it until she got out of the car. "I'll grab a cab. Hopefully, you'll be at him a while."

"We'll see," he replied. "Salerno's a tough cookie." He turned the key in the ignition. "Like somebody else I know," he added.

Agent Handler took the compliment without comment, but smiled as she got out to cross the street. Eileen wanted to walk by the precinct just to rub it in their nose. She looked at her watch. Enough time to get home and have lunch with her son. Things didn't work out so bad after all.

Jimmy Salerno wanted the location of the interview to be to his advantage. He thought about taking the Feeb to the bar or Marge's, but he didn't want the backwash it would cause. He thought about where Heather Raimondo was found and settled on the driving range. No way somebody that big was going to handle a golf club.

The owner, who was there in the mornings, gave Salerno a little salute as he did whenever he saw him. "Your partner not joining us today?" he asked.

"Nope. Somebody got to keep the City safe. Two buckets, Mike."

The beared man hoisted two wire baskets of balls up onto the counter. "You need clubs?" he asked the big black man in the gray suit.

"He's just observing. Them two buckets are for me," Jimmy answered. "We're going down the end."

"Police business, huh?"

"He's trying to sell me something, Mike, " Salerno answered.

The two of them walked down to the last point. They looked like a cartoon, the smaller, squat man carrying a golf bag and two buckets of balls and the immaculately dressed huge black walking, empty-handed behind him.

"Here's the deal, Renaldo," Salerno told him when he put his paraphernalia down. "I'm supposed to meet with you. I am meeting with you. You want to talk to me while I'm hitting my shots, talk to me. That's it."

"You going to talk back?" the agent asked.

Salerno's answer was to hit a decent drive.

"You don't like me," Dellum told him. "You don't like me because I'm black or from the Bureau. You don't like me here on your case. But we're going to get the bad guy. And no matter how we get him you're going to get the credit. Be at the press conference, whatever."

The detective put three balls in his pocket and put another down to drive.

"Look, Salerno, I need to have input from local law enforcement. We both know that ninety percent of kidnappings are by someone the children knew, usually family. And that we're probably looking at a male unsub. Women act after recent losses, such as stillbirth, miscarriage, maybe even abortion. There was a woman up here, killed her kids one after another over the years. Her name was 'Noe', right? She walked didn't she? Your Special Investigation Unit had a shot at it. I know the subject well. Take, for instance, the article in *The New England Journal of Medicine*, 'Slaughter of Innocents'. What we got here is more like the case you had, Raimondo, wasn't it?"

Salerno didn't answer and teed up another ball. Dellum went on, "Our Behavioral Unit is already working on a profile. Doing a victimology study-who the children were and what they did."

Jimmy stopped for a moment. The agent thought it was because he was going to open up or at least respond, but it was only to watch the sea gulls that had landed on the berm three hundred yards out.

R.D. tried another approach, "We respect what you've done. We know that once the initial momentum of an investigation is lost, the case goes stale, it gets stuffed in the back of the drawer. Nobody wants it but you. The Bureau is with you. And with our resources we'll help you clear this." He loosened his striped necktie. "We're probably looking at somebody in a position of trust, who knows how to deal with kids. Somebody who lives alone because of the high level of planning and risk. But you know all that. You've lived with this case, you know things that nobody else does. Together, our technology and manpower and you, it will be enough. We'll clear this case."

Jimmy Salerno didn't take the bait. His answer was to launch a long shot at the birds on the berm.

32

Rook was surprised that it took him so long to get to the address he had copied off of Lefko's blotter. It had started to rain again, a cold rain, and traffic was slow on the asphalt road.

The address was for a tract house in the last of a series of cul-de-sacs. The development, called Hilltop Farms, looked exactly like the one across the two-lane highway. There were wooden stakes in the last lot. An oval sign outside the Jelks' read: "Welcome to Our Loving Home."

Like the house across the street and the one two doors down, the Jelks' was a two-and-a-half-story with a dormer for an extra floor. Maybe a spare bedroom, a study, or a playroom. All the homes had a stone facing and chimney surrounded by stucco. Every other house was painted beige. The other homes, like 6201, were painted white with pastel trim. There were kids' toys, bikes, and big wheels in front of some of the places, but not the one he was eyeballing.

Rook parked at the top of the cul-de-sac and watched the house from his rear-view mirror while he fiddled with a clipboard. Somehow a clipboard told everybody that whoever had it was there for some good reason.

A fence coated in green plastic ran to the rear of the house. There was an open space beyond with scrub pines and brambles that seemed to slope down.

206

He saw no movement in the Jelks' place. The front light fixture was on even though it hadn't gotten dark yet, probably from the night before. A light blue station wagon backed out of its driveway next door.

Rook sat for twenty minutes then drove out of the development and then around it twice. There was a looped street in the back which accessed a stone road to a brick house in the woods. His defroster was shot and the rain came down harder and harder. Rook decided to find a place to get something to eat. Diners were good, but the better the food, the worse the information.

He drove through the storm, thinking about a meatloaf platter. Two miles up ahead, the road spread out into a four-lane highway. Rook could see a restaurant up ahead and exited.

A gas station was on one side and closest to him, a converted fast-food restaurant with a long addition and lots of metal siding. The decor was forced patriotic with red, white, and blue everywhere and machine-made prints of colonial scenes.

He sat at the counter where the chances of collecting information were increased. The manager, who also served as the host, was an overdressed Korean. The counterman was also Korean, probably eighteen or nineteen. His name tag read "Jason", and he had streaked his hair with blonde and pierced his nose. Welcome to America.

Neither the manager nor Jason had anything to say. The meatloaf that came by looked dried out. Rook ordered a combination seafood platter and succotash. The pie in the turning carousel looked good. He had a second cup of coffee. The cashier, whose name was Sonny, popped her gum and forgot to give him change.

Rook wanted to swing back to the Jelks house again to see why the detective had marked it down. The rain slowed down and he started back to the development. He noticed a tail three cars back. When he swung in and out of a gas station and jumped a red light, there was a second tail waiting for him. Who was following him would tell him something. Rook doubled back to the diner and went inside to wait.

Nobody came in. As he started out again, the rain came on heavy again. No way was he going to go back and sit on that house and listen to the pounding on his car. He went back to his room. They were waiting for him.

"Since when does Uncle Sam do B&E?"

"Who says we're the Feds?"

"You look like accountants and I didn't invite you."

"Is it a rule that all you PI's got wide mouths?" Eileen Handler asked.

"Is it a rule that you Feds got to cover every minority when you pair up?"

Dellum stretched so that Rook could see the silk lining of his six-hundred-dollar suit and his big rig .45. "You trying to jump their play, Mr. PI, that's your business. But the case is ours now so you're messing in Uncle's business. It's about business, isn't it?"

Rook knew better than to play the hard ass and ask him for a warrant. He reached over and picked up the phone. "I'll be checking out," he told the front desk.

"We appreciate that," Handler told him. "How about sending us a postcard of the Empire State Building."

Agent Dellum got up. "Nice doing business with you, Mr. Rook. I trust we'll not be seeing you again. And since you've crossed some state lines, how about you leave your firearms with me?"

Rook had no choice and put them on the dresser. He remembered the reference from the history book Rosen had given him, "1-8-3", Article One, Clause Eight, Section Three of the Constitution. You got the right to regulate my business," he said with a smirk. "I'm going to take a hot shower and then watch one of the in-room movies. I think they got J. Edgar in a bra and panties."

He went into the bathroom and started the water. When he saw the lights of their car swing away, he packed his two bags and checked out.

Leaving his Crown Victoria at the airport, he rode the train back into town where he picked up a rental. Rook knew that if he followed up on the Jelks' house again, the Feds would be there to block him. But he also knew Salerno wasn't going to back off.

He knew that Salerno had spent hundreds of nights, thousands of hours waiting for something to happen, watching a window or a door, sitting in a cold car. When the detectives were lucky, there as a chase, the rush of danger, and sometimes the exhilaration of victory. For the good cops, all of it strengthened the bond between them.

For Rook, the bond was with his phantom brother, calling, pleading with him to find the murderer. He waited for Salerno to leave his home and then followed him.

33

Detective Misher knew that it could cost his partner his gold shield if he disregarded the boss' direct order to stay out of the Jelks' case. Zinn would not let it pass if Jimmy defied him. And, the Eyes didn't fool around when it came to obstruction. On the other hand, the Inspector hadn't told him to stay out of it. As to the Feebs, there was no way those college boys would catch him doing anything. He'd scout around. Be in and out. He owed it to his partner and that came first.

It was the way the Jelks' lawn sloped down to the house in the woods that stuck with Chick. There was something wrong with that. Not the lady with the glass eye and the fourteen cats. All that weird shit didn't mean anything. It never did. Just in the movies. But there was something about the house at the end of that long hill and how the little girl must have looked to the lady in the woods. Also, he could check-out Rose Colanzi. It was stretching it looking at her again because she worked for the same doc as Heather Raimondo's mother. But he had told Jimmy he would.

Misher took a day of lost time. He told Salerno just enough so that it wouldn't ruin his stroke as he tried again to knock the gulls off that berm three hundred yards out.

He made a pass-by through the development. The Feds had a car outside the Jelks' and the view of the cat lady's house from there didn't do him any good. He had good access through Sherbrooke Circle, the circular street that looped around behind the woods. The road was a decent macadam which branched off to a utility substation and then to the right to the narrow stone access to the cat lady's house.

He took it easy going in and even thought about walking because he was in his own car and didn't want any stones bouncing up and chipping the paint. There was a thin stream with a few downed trees on the driver's side. There were no birds and he didn't see any squirrels or whatever running around, probably because of the fourteen cats.

On the right was an old pump house. Misher got out to walk up to it. He approached the clapboard structure with his weapon at his side. The small building looked abandoned and the windows were broken, but a utility line ran from the top right corner through the trees. Chick was always careful and he went in like he was hitting the house on Ann Street. The place was empty except for some discarded beer cans that had rusted out. A sheaf of newspaper was five years out of date.

As the stones on the little road got bigger, Misher left his Oldsmobile and walked the rest of the way up to the brick house. It was still some hundred yards away, but as he closed about half the distance, he could detect the rank smell of the cats. The ammonia smell got strong as he came through the woods. Three orange cats scattered as he approached the brick house.

It was a two-story structure with a detached garage. The driveway was empty. The house looked surprisingly neat.

Chick went to the garage first. The side windows were uncovered, and he could see inside. The door was unlocked.

The floor was clean, without even an old oil stain. On the left side was steel shelving that held hardware odds and ends. A scythe hung from a nail next to the shelving. Misher took it down for the moment and checked the sacks leaning against the walls. There were fifty pound bags of organic cat food and deodorizing kitty litter that obviously didn't work too well. There also was potting soil and two bags of lime.

Since lime was sometimes used in disposing of bodies, Chick took a sample and put it in one of the plastic baggies he kept in his inside jacket pocket. He had to put his weapon down to do that.

As he did, he heard the door behind him squeak open. Misher made a grab for his gun, but was unable to bring it up in firing position in a smooth motion. A coal black cat had pushed open the door and stared at him with its emerald eyes.

The detective went back to his work, examining the tools and chemicals. He found nothing. As Misher turned to leave, a car pulled up. There was only one door to the garage, and he decided to wait. The driver got out carrying a large sack.

Chick came out and flashed his badge. "Miss Coulter," he announced.

The woman had gray hair that hung to the middle of her back. Her right eye didn't seem real. "Do you have a warrant?" she demanded. "I told you before that you had to have a warrant." She did not put the canvas bag down.

"We've never met, Miss Coulter. Do you want to show me what's in the bag?"

"No, I do not. And you are trespassing since you don't have a warrant, and that's a crime. I'm going to call the police."

She dropped the sack unceremoniously and headed for the house.

"Miss Coulter. I'm here to check on your cats. We've had complaints."

The cat lady stopped in her tracks. "Complaints, complaints! You know that felines are perfectly clean."

Misher walked towards her, capturing the ground between them. "I'm here to check on their welfare, their safety. We've had complaints."

Her face became twisted with anger and a strange hue came over her sallow complexion. "Their safety, their safety. Who would dare…"

Misher walked her to the front door. "I'm sure it's a mistake, Miss Coulter."

The black cat that had been in the garage ran up on the small front porch. Two more came around the side of the house, and then a half-dozen others came out of the woods.

"Now look what you've done," the cat lady complained. "They think it's feeding time. "No, Sy. No, Jinxie. Not now. Zummer get down."

Three other cats appeared at the window. "They're the only ones that are allowed in the house. And they're not allowed out. Only Faustus here comes and goes, comes and goes."

"We frown on letting your animals run loose, but I'm not here about that. Have all of your felines had their vaccinations? I'd like to see their records."

Her bad eye seemed to roll around. "Not without some paperwork."

Chick started back to his car. "That's fine. I'll have a 'pick-up' out here tomorrow to collect them then. We can check it that way."

She wrung her hands. "No, no. I'll get the records. You wait here."

"I have to have a close-up on at least four of your animals, Miss Coulter. Your nice fellow here will do as one."

The social worker with the bad eye knew that the three inside would give the best profile and maybe that would quiet whoever had complained. She opened the front door. The first room was immaculate and smelled of potpourri. There were knit coverlets on the small sofa and the pink side chair. There was no television.

Almost at once the two of them saw the bloody cat prints that went half-way out of the kitchen and then back again. "No, no," the cat lady said as she started to run. "No, no."

Detective Misher ran after her, his weapon drawn.

"No, no," she cried. "Bad girls!" The three cats had gotten at the bag of smelts that was defrosting in the sink. Half-eaten silver fish were strewn across the floor. A gray and white cat was gnawing on one in the corner. "Shoo, shoo," the cat lady said. "That was your dinner. Shoo, Shoo."

Chick had holstered his gun as quickly as he had presented it. "Well, I guess there's no question that they have a healthy appetite. Do you have a scratching post? I hope you haven't declawed them."

"That's barbaric," Miss Coulter gasped.

"These are indoor cats? You know we frown at letting them run at large."

"Mister, I didn't get your name. May I see your identification again, please?"

"Katz, K-a-t-z. Isn't that something?" Chick said "Katz and here I am." He looked at his watch. "It is getting late, Miss Coulter. If you can get those vaccination papers for me, I'll make a quick home inspection and be on my way."

"Not without me you won't," she answered. "I'll lead the way."

The cat lady took him through her house. Misher found nothing and left. He got Jimmy Salerno on the cell phone at the driving range, "How you hittin', partner?" he asked.

"Far and straight, Chick. Far and straight."

Misher picked up some small rocks to throw at the half dozen cats running in and out of the woods. "Bullshit, Jimmy, I can hear the slice from here."

"In a pig's eye, brother."

Chick reached his car and slowly backed out of the stony lane. "Save me a bucket, I'm going to make a last pass by the Jelk's house and meet you at the range."

"Don't disturb none of them college boys, partner." Salerno teed up another ball and launched a drive at the gulls.

The Feds were still parked in the driveway, but the car was empty. A blue station wagon approached from the opposite direction. Misher could see that a small, older woman was driving. Suddenly, a black Labrador Retriever ran into the road from behind the Jelks'. It ran directly into the path of the vehicle which hit the dog broadside, knocking it into the air. The driver did not stop.

"What the fuck?" Chick said out loud. "That ain't right." The woman went into her house as if nothing had happened.

Misher called his partner back. "Jimmy," he said, "something ain't right with the Colanzi woman. I'm going in."

Salerno left the half full bucket and ran to his car. Rook was parked across the road and followed him. If anybody was going to help him close the case for the Raimondo's, it was going to be Detective Jimmy Salerno, whether he wanted to or not.

215

"Work to do, work to do," Rose Colanzi sang, without a thought about the Jelks' dog that she had just killed or little Sandy Jelks whose neck she had broken, or Heather Raimondo whom she had left by the side of the road like a bag of rocks, or the four other little girls whose parents had left their children all alone. Too busy to keep them safe, sitting in their houses counting out their money, sitting in the parlor eating bread and honey.

Misher pulled across the street. He'd check it all out. Maybe the Jelk's kid had picked up the fiber that another victim had left there. He checked the car first. It was immaculate. Chick approached the house. The back door was unlocked. As he went inside, he heard a woman singing in a thin voice. Misher followed the sound up the stairs. She was singing nursery rhymes.

The first flight of steps were carpeted and he made his ascent soundlessly. There were three wooden steps up to the closed door in the dormer. Chick had a feeling that he had many times before, that he had the bastard.

The door looked like it was a hollow core. He'd be in and on her in a minute. Follow the rules he had to, but only those. Misher started up the steps combat-ready.

The first step creaked. The singing stopped. Chick went up and in through the door like a freight train. There was an ironing board in the middle of the room. On it was a child's terry cloth robe.

Rose Colanzi was pressed in the corner behind the door. Her eyes were wild. Her lips were bubbling spit. She heard the rushing sound of a thousand pairs of beating wings. She still had the hot iron in her hand, and she hit Misher in the back of the head. The blow was upward, but she had the strength of a madwoman, and it staggered him. As he started to turn towards her, she struck him again. The blow landed at his temple and he crumpled.

She was on him like a beast, pounding him again and again, burning away his face with the searing hot metal. She hit him again and again until she was exhausted. And then she went back downstairs.

When Rose Colanzi was in her kitchen, it was as if nothing had happened. She didn't even see that her hands and clothes were wet with blood.

Jimmy Salerno put the bubble light up on his car roof and drove hard through traffic. Now! he thought. We close this case now! The pages of the Heather Raimondo murder book appeared in his head and he saw them turn faster and faster. He ran two red lights, his own lights flashing, his heart pounding.

And then his left arm hurt and his neck. It was hard for him to breathe. Salerno knew that he was having a heart attack, but he pushed on. "I've go to close this," he said. "My case, my case." He started to pass out. He pointed his car towards an open parking spot.

Rook was three cars behind and pulled up alongside. Salerno was clammy and his breathing shallow. He reached for his cell phone, but Rook took it.

"Call this in, you New York fuck. I'm having an MI."

"Where you going, Jimmy?"

"You prick, I'm having a heart attack."

"You got that, Jimmy. Where you going?"

Salerno hesitated, but he knew that Rook had him. "Next door to the Jelks'. My partner..."

"I hear ya, brother." He dialed 911. "Officer down," he said and gave the address. In moments the operator would have all available cars and the paramedics responding to the call that a cop had been shot. Lucas took Salerno's service weapon. "We're going to clear this, Salerno. We're going to clear this now."

Rose Colanzi was washing fruit at the kitchen sink when Rook came to the door. "Police," he said.

"Certainly," she answered as if she knew him. The small, dark-haired woman invited him in, with a peach still in her hand.

He didn't want trouble from Salerno's partner. "Misher," he called. "It's Lucas Rook." There was no answer. Rook walked towards the steps. The unmistakable smell of burning flesh came to him, and he started up the stairs.

The smell grew stronger and Rook moved as fast as his bad leg would allow. Rose Colanzi ran after him, her brain exploding with childhood terrors, the sound of the thousand wings in her head. The sound of the beating black wings. The sound of the gabardine habit rustling down the hall of the orphans' home so many years ago. "Who's been so bad that they're all alone?" said the nun's voice that had no mercy. "Who's been so bad that they're all alone?" Like Heather Raimondo whose mother put her aside so she could make money at Dr. Braslow's. Like Sandy Jelks whose father was always gone. Like the other ones left alone.

At the top of the first flight she was on him, jumping on his back, scratching, snarling, biting. Rook tried to shake her off, but couldn't. He threw himself against the wall, but she held fast, trying to reach around to get his eyes.

Rook had Salerno's revolver, but knew he couldn't get off a shot. He spun around twice and struck at her with his elbows, but she held fast clawing at his face. "Along came a blackbird and pecked off her nose, her nose, her nose…"

Rook moved to the edge of the stairway and, ducking his head, threw himself backwards down the steps.

Even on the carpeted stairs, the fall was enough to break Rose Colanzi's neck. Rook got up and looked at her. Her face was contorted and twitching. Her eyes were rolled back in her head.

Rook went upstairs and found Detective Misher. His face was unrecognizable. There was no pulse. When Rook saw the white child's robe on the ironing board, he knew that the animal downstairs was the killer of the little girls.

He went back down the steps to her. She was still breathing, but it was shallow and labored. He took Detective Salerno's .38, and placing the barrel to Rose Colanzi's head, he shot her twice.

Rook called Harry Raimondo, who was drinking scotch at the kitchen table while his wife slept tranquilized in their child's room.

"It's done," Lucas told him. "It's done." He thought he heard the huge man crying as he hung up the phone.

If you enjoyed

PRIVATE JUSTICE
by Richard Sand

you won't want to miss Lucas Rook in

CAPITOL PUNISHMENT

Coming soon in hardcover from Durban House Publishing

Turn the page to see what the critics have to say about Richard Sand's blockbuster thriller *Tunnel Runner* now available at your favorite bookstore or online from Amazon.com.

High Praise for Tunnel Runner

Fans of the espionage thriller genre, rejoice! The author has a keen grasp of plotting, pacing and characterization with vivid pages that jump off the page and twists that confound until the very last page...A tantalizing read enhanced by Sand's confident style.

Today's Librarian

Tunnel Runner is a fast, espionage thriller, dark and mean, but it is more than that. It has arc and poetry. *Tunnel Runner* is *The Spy that Came in from the Cold* in a turning, action nightmare. A must read.

Robert Middlemiss, *The Lofoten Run*

Richard Sand's *Tunnel Runner* is a riveting thriller, packed with action and violence. Once opened, I couldn't put it down.

Baron Bircher, *Roadhouse Blues*

Tunnel Runner will keep readers turning pages late into the night.

Rosary O'Neill, *Sweet Opium*

In his first book, *Tunnel Runner*, Richard Sand has staked out his claim in the netherworld of Ken Follett and Robert Ludlum.

Philadelphia Public Record

On the following pages is a sample chapter.

Killings

When Lorraine Knoddles returned from her sister's wedding, she called Ashman at his basecamp. He called her back. "Everything's fine," he told her.

"Good. That's nice," she answered. "You want to come for dinner on Friday?"

"Let's go out. Chinese good?"

Lorraine told him that was fine. She understood that while he was not critical of her personal life, he wasn't comfortable being around Mina Shaw.

Knoddles had seen to it that the Fulliard Stevens job was properly closed. She was paid for it and brought cash to her dinner with Ashman. Lorraine put the envelope inside her newspaper. With it was confirmation of the airfare and hotel reservations that Lorraine had made for Ashman's vacation.

"One of the remaining perks from NES," Lorraine told Ashman when she passed over the paper. "The imperialistic, capitalist conglomerate which now owns National Executive Services still gives me discounts at the New Conquistador Hotel, which they also own." Ashman thanked her. "Don't bite me or Mina," she said laughing, "but we'll being staying there too."

"As long as we don't have to have dinner together," Ashman answered, smiling. "Besides, you know I'm jealous."

They had a nice time together, and hugged good-bye.

"Sorry there's no gun-play this time, Lorraine," Ashman told her.

"Me too," she answered.

Lorraine Knoddles looked forward to the relaxed weekend. The wedding in Atlanta had been annoying. Twice she was asked about when she was going to be married. As far as she was concerned, she was.

Lorraine and Mina arrived at the hotel together.

"I got to take a run," Mina told her after they checked in. "I'll jog around the lake."

"I'll stretch out for a couple of minutes," Knoddles said, "and then start a hot bath for you."

"Love ya," Mina said as she left.

"Me too," Lorraine answered. She looked out the window, hoping she could see Mina on her run around the lake that lay in the night like a silk robe.

Ashman drove in from the airport. He was not very good at vacations, but he looked forward to seeing Maya, who was waiting for him.

Inside the hotel, a sweet love was waiting for her rendezvous. She bent, pink and nude and poured her bath salts that shimmered like pearls into the warm waiting water. The bath shone pink like the walls around it and then flashed and roared the air with hurling red fire, black smoke, white porcelain axes, and knife shards of pastel tiles.

Maya and Mina had been running around the night lake in opposite directions, towards the lake wind and away from it, crossing each other's paths and the wind that blew across the lake, running towards the waiting warmth and their love. Then they ran harder and weaker, falling as they ran, but going on, pulled down and towards their rooms and Lorraine Knoddles who exploded into the night sky.

There were flashing lights and ladders reaching up. Firemen in black suits and yellow boots were coming down to white stretchers and red and blue trucks and police that looked like they came from outer space. There were flashing lights, smoke, and howling noises, clanging noises, babbling noises, and screaming.

When Mina saw the room blown out, she knew Lorraine was dead. Mina fell down, rolling on the ground for the loss that opened and had no end. Mina knew she would never be the same. Never, ever. Mina had lost her sister, her armor, and her love and now would forever hear the clanging noises and smell the burning and see the black night turned flashing red.

Ashman watched the commotion and the destruction, counting the windows up from the ground and down from the top to see that it wasn't Maya's room, his room, her, who had been torn to pieces, and he wondered whether there was a mezzanine to count. He saw Maya walking up, turning in little circles as she did, her hands on her head like a surrendering prisoner. She was making crying sounds, and she looked lost. Maya was crying about her plants, "It's a big mess. It's a big mess," she said over and over.

"You're safe. You're safe," Ashman told her. When he took Maya to his car, he saw that she had wet herself. She was still crying and made no sense. He thought about where to take her. Ashman drove away, his windshield wipers cleaning off the fallen broken things and the little pieces of horrid, smoking jelly.

He drove out to the four lane street and onto the interstate highway. There was an Emergency Services Unit van ahead of them on the right about a hundred yards. As Ashman approached it, he thought he saw its front left tire begin to change lanes. There was a gray Ford ahead of him in his lane. The Ford was dirty and the chrome was pitted. It began to slow down and Ashman had to break.

The ESU van slowed and then came even with him. Ashman could see the two Stevens 12 gauge shot guns ready in their rack. He slid his .45 out from under his right thigh and cleared the safety, keeping it at his right hand, but away from Maya's sight or reach. "Spray and pray," he said to himself about the shotguns.

Maya could partially hear him over the radio he had put on for her. "What?" she asked, looking out the window.

Ashman didn't answer. He was getting ready for war.

The van drove off and the Ford pulled away. Ashman turned the radio up. They drove for another hour and stopped for coffee. Maya had two cups of coffee and smoked a half-dozen cigarettes, leaving one or two of them still burning. She calmed down as they drove on and wanted to talk about what had happened.

"What, is it me?" she asked. "Did anybody get killed? Did it have something to do with me? After all," she said finally, "we're making that thing."

Ashman lost his patience. "Jesus, Maya," he told her. "It's not the fucking Manhattan Project you're working on. What you're doing is lab stuff. If anybody thought what you were doing was important enough, they'd wait until you had something worthwhile and then they'd steal it, not kill you. Maybe the hotel explosion was a gas leak or maybe the Iraqi's, or those fertilizer patriots or the ghost of Christmas Past. Maybe an insane textile salesman. You're safe. You're safe. Let's find a place to drink some gin and take a swim. Everything will be fine. It is fine. Maybe we'll find a good Italian restaurant. Chicken cacciatore? Think about that."

Maya said, "Yes." She felt better knowing Ashman wasn't worried. Maybe they would have a vacation after all. She curled up and wrapped her feet in his jacket that he had put over her to keep her warm.

As they drove on, the Ford appeared again, coming up on them from behind with the lights flashing in its grill. Ashman knew that he was speeding, so he slowed. He put the .45 back under his right thigh and pulled to the shoulder of the road.

The Ford came up behind, but far enough back to pull around if it had to. The Emergency Services Unit with the shotguns was nowhere in sight. Ashman waited with battle contingencies in his mind.

There were two men inside the car. The swarthy one got out and walked up to Ashman with his badge out. The other was on the radio. Ashman could see that the one coming up wore cheap clothes and cop's shoes. He looked like a plainclothes, except the walk didn't look quite right.

"Stay in your vehicle, please," the swarthy one told them. He approached Ashman's vehicle holding up his shield. He was wearing a Smith and Wesson Model .49. "Can I see your license, registration and proof of insurance?" he asked.

Ashman showed him an impeccable, but phony Cleveland Police I.D. along with his license.

The cop, whose name was Tarkanian, looked tired and was glad to accept the badge. He had that "too many shifts for too many days" look. He talked about what was going on, the other plainclothes still hanging back in the Ford and smoking. "We don't know whether we're in the shit or it's a gas leak," Tarkanian said. "But you were coming from the scene pretty f-ing fast. My partner, Steyr's dad, was 'on the job' in Cleveland," he went on, "Maybe he'll want to say 'yo.'"

Tarkanian walked back to his partner, who was leaning against the Ford. Steyr came over. He walked like a cop. He was big and freckled and had his sleeves rolled up. Ashman couldn't see a side-arm. He was probably wearing a pancake holster in the back.

The two cops passed each other on the way. Steyr took a cigarette from his shirt pocket and threw it to his partner, who lit up and smoked, while Ashman and Steyr bullshitted for a couple of minutes about "the job" and Cleveland and the fucking Cleveland Browns and how they should rot in hell.

Steyr wished him a safe trip. Tarkanian was up ahead by the Ford and Steyr was walking back when Ashman saw him start to step across with his right foot. His right arm was moving to his holster.

Ashman hit his horn and slammed his car into reverse. "Down! Get down!" he told Maya, reaching over to push her. As Steyr pivoted with his gun out, Ashman fired four shots. One shot was high and missed, but the others were good, hitting the target in the thigh, chest, and throat. Steyr got two rounds off. One narrowly missed Maya.

Tarkanian was pounding out shots as Ashman drove at him full speed ahead. Tarkanian emptied his revolver and was speedloading as he ran bowlegged for the cover of the Ford. Ashman ran him down and shot him dead.

Maya was screaming, and their windshield was shot out. She was throwing herself around, and her forehead was bleeding from glass splinters. She was shivering. Ashman tried to calm her but she went on. "Home, home. Take me home," Maya said over and over.

"We're going home now," Ashman told her. He took her to the Ford because their windshield was gone. Maya tried to pull away. Ashman grabbed her by the wrist and brought her to him in a 'come-along' lock.

Her eyes were wide as they drove away. She was rocking back and forth. Ashman listened to the car's scanner while Maya smoked Steyr's cigarettes. Maya thought she was back home and going on a trip.

Ashman knew the Ford wasn't right. He knew that someone was coming after him and that he had to put Maya somewhere . Then he could either disappear or go for the enemy's heart, wherever that was. He wanted to take her home, but Ashman knew that whoever they were could just as easily let her go, triangulate for him, and slit her throat later.

He thought about leaving Maya in front of the Liberty Bell. He would find himself a high tree like he had in-country in Nam, in so far he was behind everybody, living in the crooks of branches, drinking the rain. He'd climb down and go rushing through the tunnels to come up and kill the enemy in their sleep. Ashman had the radio all the way up and Maya was rocking back and forth. He felt the rush of battle and was glad for it.

They passed four more highway exits. Ashman turned off at the fifth. He found a motel and checked in. There was a package store across the road and Ashman got tonic, ice, and Blue Sapphire gin. They sat together on the tan sofa next to the bed. She leaned against him and talked and smoked and drank gin until she fell asleep. He took a quick shower with the bathroom door open.

Two hours later, Ashman took her out to the SUV he had stolen. As they drove off, he told her they were going for a swim. Maya fell asleep, dreaming of them sitting in the waves.